"You can still change your mind about the deal." Cade said quietly. "Are you sure you want me to stay?"

Rusty nodded. She brought her hand to his chin and rubbed her fingertips along the rough stubble of his beard.

Cade waited, willing himself not to move.

Her fingers slid down his cheek, around his chin, and circled his lips. He was like stone—immobile, tense. She had the feeling that if he ever let go, she'd be caught up in the fury of his release like a prairie fire fanned by a crosswind. Down his chin, along his neck to the opening of his shirt, her fingers moved, slowly, as if she were measuring the strength of his will.

Heat, more heat, boiling heat was flowing across every nerve ending in her body. She knew only that she was on fire, and that the man she was touching was chiseled ice beneath her touch.

"What are you afraid of, Cade McCall?"

"You, myself, us." He couldn't take his eyes off her. He watched as her breathing quickened, her lips trembled, her eyes widened. "Don't do this, Rusty. Not unless you want me to lose control."

"Why should I spare you? I've already lost mine."

Abruptly he reached out, slid his thigh between her legs, and jerked her forward as he crushed her lips savagely beneath his. He held her against him, arching her body into his as he shattered her with the power of his desire. He was claiming all, and she was giving all—at last. . . .

WHAT ARE *LOVESWEPT* ROMANCES?

They are stories of true romance and touching emotion. We believe those two very important ingredients are constants in our highly sensual and very believable stories in the *LOVESWEPT* line. Our goal is to give you, the reader, stories of consistently high quality that may sometimes make you laugh, sometimes make you cry, but are always fresh and creative and contain many delightful surprises within their pages.

Most romance fans read an enormous number of books. Those they truly love, they keep. Others may be traded with friends and soon forgotten. We hope that each *LOVESWEPT* romance will be a treasure—a "keeper." We will always try to publish

LOVE STORIES YOU'LL NEVER FORGET
BY AUTHORS YOU'LL ALWAYS REMEMBER

The Editors

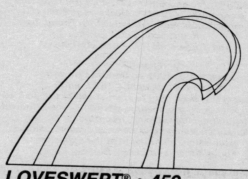

LOVESWEPT® · 459

Sandra Chastain
Firebrand

BANTAM BOOKS
NEW YORK · TORONTO · LONDON · SYDNEY · AUCKLAND

FIREBRAND

A Bantam Book / March 1991

If you would be interested in receiving protective vinyl
covers for your Loveswept books, please write to this address
for information:

Loveswept
Bantam Books
P.O. Box 985
Hicksville, NY 11802

ISBN 0-553-44103-5

Published simultaneously in the United States and Canada

PRINTED IN THE UNITED STATES OF AMERICA

OPM 0 9 8 7 6 5 4 3 2 1

With appreciation to the State of Utah Travel Council, the Executive Staff at the Little America Hotel and Towers,
and most especially to
Pauline S. Biesinger and the staff of Coldwell Banker Premier, Inc. who furnished me with information about the lovely state of Utah.

One

Rusty Wilder peeled off her dusty black Stetson and slapped it against her thigh as she entered the Salt Lake City airport. Her nerves were tied in knots over the coming meeting with Cade McCall.

She was late. And she wasn't at all certain that the choice she'd made had been wise. She'd had a number of replies to her advertisement. Many of the applicants were obviously not the caliber of man she was looking for. They were eliminated right away. Three possibles she'd turned over to a detective agency in Salt Lake City for investigation. Cade McCall, the man she was meeting, was the best of the respondents.

Rusty took a deep, ragged breath. She felt cold, even inside the heated airport. She knew the icy spot she felt in the pit of her stomach was from the nagging doubt that she might be making a mistake. She was about to take the biggest gamble of her life. From the outside, she appeared to be a tough, self-sufficient woman, but deep inside she was scared to death.

The only thing she was sure of was that it was March, the start of the breeding season on Silverwild Ranch, when a rancher counted the calves born during the past winter and made plans for the coming year.

By fall a new bull, imported from Africa, would be changing the future of her herd. And if today's meeting went right, she would have a husband by her side, changing the future of Silverwild.

If Walt Wilder were alive, Rusty was certain that he'd disapprove of his daughter running an ad to find a man. But Rusty knew what she was doing. Oh, there'd been plenty of men willing to marry Walt Wilder's daughter ten years ago, and even more now, eager to marry Ben Middleton's widow.

But none of them met her criteria. Silverwild was hers, and she intended to run it her way, without interference from anyone—including a husband. Her father had told her often enough that she would never be a beauty queen but she could be the best rancher in the state. She'd believed him on both counts, even if he had doubted her in the end. Well, she'd show him. She'd show them all.

On his deathbed, Walt Wilder had asked for two promises from Rusty, his only child. The first was that she would marry his partner, Ben. The second, that she'd have children.

Rusty had tried to keep those promises. The marriage, however, had been a mistake. Ben tried to be a real husband to her, but he could never see her as a woman or grant her an equal voice in running Silverwild. To Ben, Rusty had always been Walt's girl, practically his own. But the worst part for Rusty had been Ben's limited imagination and his reluctance to take chances. Their eight-year marriage had left Silverwild stagnant and Rusty childless.

A husband like Cade McCall would solve both her problems, Rusty reasoned. He'd father her children and stand between her and the other ranchers who derided her unconventional ideas. Yet Cade McCall would be an employee, with no say in running the ranch.

Granted, McCall or one of the other candidates was being hired for more duties than the typical wrangler. But her business was breeding cattle, and she tried to think of the arrangement strictly in those terms. McCall was a man, of course, and not a prize bull. The end result, however, would be the same. And quickly, she hoped. At thirty-two, Rusty had started to think about her biological clock running out.

Could McCall turn her down? Maybe he'd take one look at her and run the other way. She'd neither sent a picture nor asked for one in return. She had meant to clean herself up for their first meeting, but tending a sick cow all morning had left her no time to change her clothes or wrestle with her hair. But perhaps it was better to meet him looking this way, leaving the man no illusions.

She knew by now that her looks didn't exactly inspire male fantasies. She was too tall and too outspoken. Her red hair was wild, and her long, lean body not quite the softly curving female ideal men desired. Ben had been her only real lover. Then, after about a year of marriage, his heart trouble put an end to their infrequent sessions of lovemaking.

Rusty just didn't know how to play man-woman games and didn't intend to start learning now. McCall didn't have to fall in love with her, she reasoned. He didn't even have to like her. All he had to do was agree to her proposition. What red-blooded oil-field roustabout would pass up a chance to marry one of the wealthiest women in Utah and own twenty-five percent of the biggest cattle ranch in the state?

Not Cade McCall. She'd be willing to bet on it. His reply to her ad had been short and to the point. He needed a job and a home for the daughter he was raising on his own. Beyond that, Rusty knew only that he was thirty-seven years old and in good physical health. Raised in Tennessee, he had enlisted in the coast guard out of high school. He was stationed in South Carolina and Washington State. After the service, he worked his way to Alaska, ending up with a job on the pipeline.

He'd never been to Utah and knew nothing about ranching—a definite plus in Rusty's book. His six-year-old daughter, Pixie, was also an unexpected bonus. Rusty was sure McCall would see that Silverwild was a wonderful place to raise a child.

Cade McCall would not turn her down. She would explain it all to him in just the right way. Even the part about giving her children. She would deal it straight to him. The winning cards were all in her hand, she reminded herself. She was the one in control here.

She swallowed hard and studied the few people

milling around the airport waiting room. Where was he?

Across the concourse Cade McCall was asking himself the very same question about his prospective employer. Then the staccato tap of boots on the polished floor attracted his attention. The woman who came into view was a stunning eyeful. He watched her stop and pull off a dusty black Stetson, her mass of red hair falling tousled and wild across her shoulders. Cade had to catch himself from sighing out loud.

She seemed to be looking for someone but had taken no notice of him yet. He didn't mind. He was savoring his chance to take in every inch of her with an unguarded stare. Her green eyes were full of fire, the kind that could burn a man alive. A fleece-lined denim jacket ended just above a pair of jean-clad legs that would be the envy of any Las Vegas show girl. She turned her long, graceful body slowly, scanning the room.

Then Cade sighed. The gorgeous redhead sure wasn't looking for him. The woman he'd come here to meet was probably sixty-five and built like a Mack truck. She probably had a face that could stop a clock. Not one like the redhead's that could bewitch a man for a lifetime.

No matter. Cade knew he had little choice about taking this job if it was offered. His mind ran back over the ad:

Utah widow with large cattle ranch offers home and permanent employment with future advancement to single, divorced, or widowed man meeting certain qualifications. Mutually agreeable contract after six-month trial period. No experience necessary. Children welcome.

That had been the clincher. A home for Pixie and a job for himself, with "no experience necessary."

He had just made the last payment on his ex-wife's funeral, bringing his bank account to rock bottom. It seemed the right thing to do. Janie had been his wife once, and she was his child's mother. He'd also had medical bills to pay, some of Janie's and some for Pixie's last attack of bronchitis and pneumonia. The child had to be moved to a milder climate. But moving anywhere took cash. He was flat broke and tense as a grizzly bear waking up from hibernation.

Finding the ad seemed like a stroke of luck, even though he had his suspicions about the wording. Cade suspected the woman was looking for a husband, even if she didn't say so. Another reason the redhead could not be looking for him. A woman like that would never need to put herself up on the auction block. She was no loved-starved widow who had to advertise in a farm journal for a husband.

The redhead continued her slow searching look around the room. When her gaze finally crossed his, she visibly took in a quick breath. Cade felt the intensity of her stare, a connection sizzling between them like northern lights flashing in a midnight sky.

Maybe he'd been in the wilderness too long. It had been a long time since a woman's mere glance had set off such a powerful reaction. He felt his body tighten, pulling taut as a bowstring, holding him in place. Like two wild animals, wary and suspicious, they measured each other from a distance for a long tense moment.

Then she began to walk toward him. Could he hope? Could he dream? She stood inches away, and still he didn't dare to believe this breathtaking vision was his very own "Utah widow."

"McCall?" she finally asked him. Fighting back the urge to turn and run, she gave him a nervous half-smile and held out her hand.

Cade was stunned. She had a husky bedroom voice that was unexpected but suited her perfectly.

He stepped forward, removed his glove, and shook her hand. There was no disguising the firmness of her grip or the hesitant quiver in her fingertips.

"I'm McCall," he said simply.

"I'm Rusty Wilder. Let's go."

How could he have been so wrong? A Mack truck? A face that could stop a clock? Stunned, he couldn't seem to settle on anything except the fire in her red hair and the flicker of unease in her eyes.

He nodded, picked up his duffel bag, and followed her to the airport exit.

"My plane is right over there," she said, pointing to a trim white Cessna 152 that was parked nearby. It had red stripes and the word *Silverwild* painted across the side in silver.

"You can toss your bag in the back," Rusty told him as she opened the passenger-side door. She walked around the other side and climbed into the pilot seat, thankful for the momentary distraction of preparing for takeoff.

She knew that the meeting would be awkward at first. But no past experience with an employee interview had prepared her to handle a man like Cade McCall.

He was dressed in jeans, workboots, and a leather bomber jacket with the collar turned up around his neck. A black baseball cap covered his head and shaded his dark eyes, the kind Rusty knew a woman could easily get lost in. His heavy five-o'clock shadow might have been unattractive on another man, but on McCall it only served to accentuate the masculinity of a disturbingly handsome face.

Some wild, untamed element vibrated from within him, like the sound of an echo in a blind canyon. Rusty had sensed it the moment their gazes met. Unlike every other man she'd ever known, he looked at her without blinking, and he didn't ask questions.

No question about it. Cade McCall was a dangerous man. His presence so close beside her in the plane's small cabin quite simply took her breath away. He was too male, too intense, too much man for a woman without worldly experience. Clearly, he could and would hold his own—even gain the upper hand if she allowed him to. How on earth would she handle him?

McCall settled himself in the seat beside her and watched as she pitched her Stetson in back. Rusty crammed a headset over her wild hair and ran through the takeoff checklist. "Belt on?" she asked McCall over the engine's rising sound.

"Yes, ma'am." He nodded. His tone was obliging, his grin insolent. Rusty felt him watching her every move but turned her full attention back to the controls.

She cleared with the tower, taxied the plane down the runway, and took off. In the seat beside her, McCall appeared relaxed and unconcerned.

"Pretty smooth," he said finally. "How long have you been flying?"

"Since I was about sixteen. My father taught me."

"Taught you good," McCall replied with an approving nod.

Rusty glanced at him with a half-smile. Then she was annoyed with herself for being pleased by McCall's small compliment. She knew she was a good pilot; she didn't need some down-and-out drifter to tell her she was.

She guessed that Cade McCall limited his praise. He was certainly not big on small talk. That suited Rusty fine. She hadn't much patience for idle conversation and knew she wouldn't last long with a man who was full of questions. Acceptance was a rare quality and in this case, very necessary.

Cade, too, was content with silence. Perhaps it was because he hadn't had many people to talk to lately or perhaps because by nature he was spare with his words. He merely waited. When the woman was ready to talk, she would.

His fellow workers had found him distant. He was simply slow to trust. He'd been betrayed by the people he'd cared for most, his father the first to abandon him, Janie the last to leave. He swore then that he'd never care about anything or anybody again.

Cade hadn't counted on a little girl's love to break through the wall he'd built around himself.

But she had, and she'd made Eugene, the pipeline camp cook, a part of their lives too. Leaving them behind, even temporarily, had been harder than Cade had expected.

The sun was setting, though it still hung just above the horizon. Bright streaks of gold and pink hovered above mountains that looked like black teeth capped with white. They'd been flying for nearly twenty minutes. Finally the woman turned toward him.

"We're over the Silverwild spread now, McCall. You can see the cattle below, the white ones. They're Charbray."

"Sounds like French wine."

"You're not too far wrong. The Charbray comes from breeding the Charolais, which is a white cow of French origin, with the Brahman bull."

"Kinda like merging Paris, France, and Paris, Texas. Interesting idea." About like you and me, Cade thought wryly. "Why would you want to cross an ugly creature like that Brahman with anything?"

"Oh, but the Brahmans are more heat resistant, because of their well-developed sweat glands. Looks aren't important here on the Silverwild. It's the final product that we're interested in, which is what we ought to talk about before we reach the ranch house. We'll use this time to review our mutual goals."

Cade lifted his chin and glanced over the edge of the plane at the barren landscape below. "'Mutual Goals'? The ad didn't say anything about goals—mutual or otherwise. What kind of job interview is this?"

"This isn't precisely a job interview, McCall.

There are . . . certain things you need to know."

"Yes, like what kind of quarters are you providing for my daughter and me, and why do we need a contract? If I do my job, pay me. If I don't, deduct this plane ticket from my salary and fire me."

He didn't know why he was being so sharp. The woman was entitled to handle her interview any way she wanted to. It was her money. Some perverse need to rattle her calm had put him on edge. He looked over at her and tried a half-smile.

Don't let him get to you, Rusty, she told herself. This is your game. You set the rules. Just don't look at him as you lay them out.

"I don't like to waste time, McCall. I like to make the right decision the first time. For now, I'll have to say that you seem fit enough. Looks can be deceiving, of course. The job will make certain physical demands on you that might be—unusual. I simply want you to know what the future potential of your—employment might be."

He might have believed her calm except for the tightness in her voice and the flicker of uncertainty in her eyes. She still hadn't explained the exact nature of these "unusual" physical demands, and Cade could not prevent his imagination from running wild.

He nodded, forcing himself to concentrate on the landscape instead of the generous curve of her flannel shirt.

"Are physical examinations part of the deal?" he asked playfully, surprising himself with the question.

Rusty gave him a quick, startled glance, then pulled her eyes away. "No. But they are important to my plans."

Cade didn't consider himself a man to whom social banter came easily, and this talk of physical examinations was more than suggestive. He was willing to bet that her pulse was running just as rampant as his own. Still, such control in a woman was rare.

"I assure you, Miss Wilder, I am in perfect physical condition. I had a checkup just last month."

"I know."

"You know?" This time Cade couldn't control his reaction. "What does that mean?" he asked point-blank.

"It means I had you checked out before I sent the ticket, McCall. You have a six-year-old daughter with a chronic bronchial condition, but your health is perfect."

However, she didn't add that it was important to her plans to make certain that the child's condition wasn't the result of a hereditary weakness in the McCall line. "And it's 'Mrs. Wilder,'" she said instead. "I never took my husband's name."

"You never took your husband's name, but it's Mrs., not *Ms.*," he said dryly. "At least you're not one of those card-carrying, men-bashing feminists.

"On the contrary, Mr. McCall. I'm very much a feminist. But I'm also a realist. Whether or not I like men isn't the issue. This employment is a business agreement, pure and simple. But it has to be an amenable arrangement for my plans to work. I intend to be fair. I'll do everything possible to see that it offers as much to you as you will offer to me."

"Just out of curiosity, how'd you get confidential medical records?"

"Truthfully, I have no idea. I didn't ask. I simply employed a person who's in the business of getting hold of such things."

"And what else do you know about me?"

"I know that your wife died after an extended illness brought on by her addiction to alcohol and prescription drugs. I know that you're responsible enough to have paid off all her hospital bills and funeral expenses, even though she left you nearly seven years ago. Foolish, but admirable. Loyalty is a rare trait. I also know you were unaware you had a daughter until after your wife's death. And I know you're flat broke. Is that about it?"

"Just about. But I'm beginning to think you know something that I don't. When am I going to learn the rest of the story? What exactly do *you* expect to get out of this?"

"I had planned to wait until we got to the ranch before explaining all the details, but I suppose it doesn't matter. You'll have to know sooner or later."

"Know what, Mrs. Wilder? Your dark, mysterious reason for hiring me? I'll bet I've already figured that out, but I'm not sure it's legal."

"What I expect to get," she blurted out, turning toward him in quick surprise "is a temporary husband, Cade McCall." Rusty heard herself and cringed. This wasn't going the way she'd planned. Blast the man, he wasn't even reacting.

After a long silence she forced herself to regain her composure and speak calmly. "I had planned to discuss the terms of your employment after you'd seen the ranch. I thought you'd be more agreeable then."

Husband? Cade's expression might have remained unchanged, but his inner reaction was of complete disbelief. His only comment was a strained "So, Eugene was right."

"Eugene? Who is he?"

"Eugene is Pixie's friend, the base-camp cook who first saw your ad." Suddenly the air became tense. "He warned me that this might happen. Go on, Mrs. Wilder, tell me the rest. I don't think I can wait for the tour."

She might as well. Her inability to control her response to the man had ruined her calm, businesslike approach. Like some love-struck teenager she'd blurted out her plan and made herself look like an idiot. Well, she had no choice now but to go on.

"I'll make few demands on your time," she added hurriedly. "Once we're married, you're free to come and go, so long as you remember that you're a Wilder and conduct yourself accordingly."

"A Wilder?" All the tension simmering just beneath the surface suddenly caught fire and erupted. Cade sat up, narrowed his lips, and spit out his response, one knife-sliced word at a time. "Not on your life, boss-lady. The name is McCall, the same as yours will be if we should get married, which is, I might add, highly unlikely at this point. Even if I accepted your proposal, I have a child who needs a mother, not a ranch foreman.

"In addition," he went on tightly, "I like to drink, play poker, and make love to a woman now and then. What sort of terms do you intend to write into that contract to take care of my personal needs?"

Cade didn't bother to add that those pastimes

had been discarded years ago in the aftermath of his divorce.

"Perhaps you should see Silverwild first, before we try to iron out the fine points," Rusty said smoothly.

Ignoring the tense silence, Rusty banked the plane, circling the mountains to the south. Cade McCall was a hard man to decipher. He hadn't said no, but he didn't seem to be receptive to the idea of marriage either.

But wasn't that what she wanted? A six-month trial period where they could work out the details and decide whether or not marriage was to their mutual advantage?

Cade's strongest objection so far was over the issue of changing his name. Well, she could make that worth his while. Cash flow was limited since she'd bought the new bull, but outside of her banker, nobody else knew. And a few well-chosen stud fees for the bull would change all that.

By the time the other ranchers got over the shock of her new bull, she and Cade would be well on her way to working out the more personal part of their future plans. The truth was, it didn't matter what the man's name was or what name appeared on the marriage certificate. Once Cade McCall married Rusty Wilder, he would be a Wilder, whether he wanted to admit it or not.

McCall was a definite surprise. He didn't seem to be a typical drifter or some fortune hunter looking for a free ride. She was prepared for him to demand concessions of his own. She just didn't know what those concessions would be. However, she knew that in order to stand up to Cade McCall, she'd have to deal with him directly. No guile, no feminine wiles—not that such maneuvers had ever been Rusty's style.

"I know this seems like an impossible proposition, McCall, but if you will be patient until after dinner, I think I'll be able to assure you that Silverwild will satisfy all your needs."

"Oh? That ought to be interesting."

She ignored the implication of his words. "Now if you'll look below, I'm going to take a quick pass around the spread so that you can get an idea of what I'll be offering the man I choose. And you're right, it isn't a foregone conclusion that it will be you. You may not be able to handle the terms of my agreement."

"Oh I can handle them, Ms. Wilder. As long as you are prepared to give as much as you get. Don't you worry about that. The question is whether or not I *choose* to."

The plane bobbled for just a second, and Cade felt an immense glow of self-satisfaction that he'd broken through her steely reserve again. She might appear as cold as one of those snow-covered peaks below, but so did Mount St. Helens until she erupted. Then the entire Northwest felt her heat.

"Another thing you're right about, ma'am," he added carelessly. "Just like you said earlier, appearances can be deceiving. But passion? That's something a person can never completely disguise. I'm looking forward to dinner—and learning how you intend to satisfy my needs."

Two

She came up behind him on the patio like a shadow.

"Well, does what you've seen of the ranch come up to your expectations?"

"I had no expectations," Cade answered honestly. "But if I had, I would never have envisioned all this." He had thought he was alone until he heard her speak. Being caught unaware bothered him; it rarely happened. The woman was disturbing, not only to his peace of mind but to his senses.

From the time their eyes had met in the airport, the tension had grown. Rusty's plan to show him what she had to offer had in no way changed that. Their plane had circled the house, farm buildings, and herds of cattle grazing across the pastureland. She landed on a private airfield that stretched across the flat landscape and ended at a hangar that housed the plane and several pieces of farm equipment. They climbed into a waiting Jeep that Rusty Wilder drove fast but expertly to the white stucco ranch house.

The setting sun caught the red roof tiles of the house, turning them the same fire-shot color as Rusty's hair. She drove around to the side of the horseshoe-shaped house and came to a stop just inside the courtyard. For a moment she stared at the steering wheel, relaxing her grasp one finger at a time before leaning back and letting out a deep breath.

The sun dropped behind the mountains in the distance as if a curtain had been lowered. In March the air was still cold, and with the moon covered by a blanket of clouds, the night sky turned volcano-black.

"We're here, McCall."

That was the extent of her conversation. Cade nodded and followed her inside. A plump gray-haired woman identified as Letty led him up the center stairs to the upper level and down the curved hallway to the left.

"You're in the guest wing of the house," she explained. "Rusty's room is opposite yours, across the courtyard in the other wing." After taking a long assessing look at Cade, she smiled and nodded as if in approval. She told him that dinner would be served in forty-five minutes and left the room.

He might have told her that he hadn't expected a ranch hand applying for a job to be invited to have dinner with the owner, but he wasn't just any hired hand. He was auditioning as a husband.

Cade allowed himself for a moment to wonder exactly what Rusty Wilder had in mind. The kind of experience she was seeking wasn't something he could put on a job application. And there were no references to be checked. Mrs. Wilder would have to take a calculated risk. Or ask for a demonstration.

That thought set his blood pulsating and refused to be dismissed. Cade felt his body begin to react. He should have gone into Fairbanks a day early. But the only woman he'd known intimately had married last year. Until now, he'd thought that he'd closed off that part of his life. He groaned.

There wasn't even a snowbank nearby to plunge into. A cold shower would have to do. Then he'd take a look in his bag. Eugene had packed it, and knowing Eugene's eclectic taste, its contents might prove to make the evening even more interesting.

The private bathroom offered both a Jacuzzi and a shower. He choose the shower, crossing his fingers that the water was cold and the pressure firm. He wasn't disappointed. An electric razor was plugged into the wall, and he used it. He wondered if it had been placed there for him or if some other occupant had left it behind.

When he returned to his bedroom, he found a pair of dark slacks and a gray striped shirt laid out on his bed, new clothes that he'd never seen before. Even Eugene hadn't gone this far.

Cade picked up the shirt and fingered the soft finish of the fabric—expensive, imported. He frowned. The woman wasn't kidding when she said that she was offering him employment with special privileges. He was being bought, from the skin out. And Cade McCall was not now and never had been for sale. He'd earn his own way, for himself and for Pixie—somehow or other.

Cade emptied his duffel bag and sighed with relief. Eugene's choices were good. He found a fresh blue chambray shirt and a clean pair of jeans. His only concession to formality was donning the new pair of sleek black running shoes he'd bought in Fairbanks before he left.

Closing the last button, he stepped out onto the veranda circling the second floor of the house. It was cold outside, but he was used to it. He needed it. In the distance he could hear the soft lowing of cattle that he could no longer see. Creeping up the posts below were brown vines that would bring colorful sweet-smelling flowers when the weather warmed. And in the enclosed courtyard beneath the porch he could hear the sound of water running in a fountain. This kind of luxury seemed about as out of place against the stark Utah landscape as he did.

The expensive perfume worn by the woman standing behind him was out of place too.

Rusty didn't speak. Her ability to sustain silence was unnerving. He'd never met a woman who didn't feel the need to fill an awkward space with chatter. This one simply waited. But he could feel her eyes on his back. He couldn't see what she was wearing, and he fought the urge to turn around. After a long silence he said, "Silverwild ranch is impressive. Your husband must have been a man of vision to carve all this out of a desert."

"It was my father, and he was more than that. He lived for this ranch—and me, of course. His only disappointment was that he produced only one child."

"I suppose he wanted a son, to inherit all this?"

"He never said so. I don't think he ever doubted my ability to handle whatever needed handling."

But he had, she admitted in that secret part of herself that she managed to seal off most of the time. He wasn't certain that she was strong enough to follow his dream. That's why he took Ben in as a partner, grooming him to take over. Her father hadn't realized that Ben was only a shadow of himself. She'd known, but she had never been able to oppose her father's wishes. So she'd married a man twenty years her senior because her father had asked her to. Of course she hadn't expected Ben to have a heart attack during the first year of their marriage and live out his remaining years as a quarrelsome housebound invalid.

McCall was both commanding and disturbing. Not at all like her husband in temperament or character. Cade McCall was his own man, and she knew without a doubt that though she might buy him, she'd never own him.

"Letty will serve dinner in five minutes, McCall. Don't be late. Letty doesn't allow that from anybody. I wouldn't advise you to make an enemy of her."

Cade heard a silken swish, then silence.

He threaded his fingers through his hair. ↓ was right. He should have turned and greeted h. Perversity was both childish and demeaning. I was being interviewed for a job, a job that provided a home for his child. Nothing more. She was giving him six months to decide how permanent it would be. He certainly didn't have to marry her. Nothing was going to pay as well as pipeline work, but being a wealthy man had never mattered much. If a job on the ranch didn't work out, at least he'd have Pixie in a better place while he had time to find something else.

A few minutes later he was following the sound of Rusty's voice as she gave directions to Letty. He found her in the large room in the center of the house that formed the inner curve of the U-shaped structure. Large overstuffed cream-colored couches circled a massive rock fireplace where a fire roared red and orange in the hearth.

She was standing in the shadows, the scent of her perfume exciting his senses once again. By the time he took a good look at her, Cade had the strong feeling that he should skip dinner altogether. His insides churned as if he'd already eaten locoweed.

She was wearing her hair pulled back by silver combs. Her dress was loose and long, like the kind some island woman might have worn after the coming of the missionaries. With a high neckline and full sleeves it was designed to conceal. The imagination, however, was more stimulating than any open physical display, and Cade quickly decided that Mrs. Wilder's gown was the most provocative garment he'd ever seen. Its shimmering color was the same shade as her hair, the color of fire. Tiny little mirrors were stitched across the shoulders and around the hem. Every movement reflected a hundred shimmering flames that licked out at him with every breath she took.

"So, what's the deal, Mrs. Wilder?" he asked in a clipped voice.

"Not yet, McCall. Dinner first. Then business."

"You know, there's no way in hell I can sit across

from you and eat without being told what this is all about."

"Oh, I think you can. I think you can probably do whatever you set your mind to, McCall."

She turned and led the way into a dining room only a fraction smaller than the great room. She hoped she'd put enough distance between them to help her control her own turbulent emotions.

A long dark wooden table that could have seated a dozen people had been set for two, one plate at one end, one at the other. A brass chandelier cast soft light across the room.

Cade glanced at the arrangement and smiled. She wasn't taking any chances. She wasn't going to explain a thing until she was ready and knew how to protect herself.

Holding out her chair, he waited until she sat down. When his hands grazed her shoulders, he was rewarded with a slight start, then absolute stillness, and a measured "Thank you."

At the other end of the table, Cade unfolded his napkin and waited as Letty appeared from the kitchen with a tureen of soup.

"Nice—whatever that is you're wearing," he said, and began to eat his soup. "The mirrors seem to set you on fire."

She didn't answer. She didn't know what to say. He was the first man she'd met who hadn't been in awe of her. And she admitted that wearing the red-orange gown had been a perverse attempt to rattle his composure. She couldn't be certain what she'd accomplished because he was so adept at hiding his emotions.

A small salad replaced the soup.

"You're not quite what I expected," Rusty finally admitted as the salad plates were removed.

He looked up. Even from his end of the table he could feel a certain wavering in her bearing. Her fiery appearance and her cool demeanor seemed in disagreement with each other, and he wondered if he might be sending out the same mixed signals. "Oh? Your report leave out something?"

It left out what kind of man you are, she could have said. It didn't tell her how difficult this would be, nor did it suggest how uncertain she'd feel in his presence.

The main course of vegetables and rare roast beef was a diversion that Rusty used to the fullest while she collected her erratic thoughts and replied, "No, the report was rather complete. Now it's my turn. Why did you answer my ad?"

"Like you told me," he said, watching the main course being replaced by a kind of custard with cinnamon sprinkled on top, "food first, business later. By the way, ma'am," he complimented Letty as she refilled his glass with wine, "you're a very good cook. This meal is a definite improvement over the cooking I'm used to."

Letty didn't try to control her smile of appreciation. "Thank you, young man. You look like you could use a good meal or two. You're too thin. Don't they feed you up there in the wilderness?"

"Alaska isn't all wilderness, ma'am. But we don't get food like this as troubleshooters out on the pipeline. Our cook, Eugene, is into beans, bacon, and biscuits. He doesn't have much imagination and"—he glanced at Rusty—"he certainly isn't much for stimulating dinner conversation."

"Humph!" Letty said with a sharp look at Rusty.

"I expect that he'd be an improvement over eating with a person who seems to have forgotten good conversation is the leavening for a good meal, not to mention the measure of her upbringing."

"Letty! We'll have coffee in the study."

"Yes, ma'am," Letty said in a tone of exaggerated servitude. "But you—" she leaned down and whispered in Cade's ear, "you sneak back into the kitchen later, and I'll leave a nice piece of pie in the fridge for you."

"Icebox pie, no doubt," he said with a wink.

"Not on your life, sugar. It's fresh apple—make my own crust too." Letty paused and looked at Rusty. "Willadean used to like it best of all, before she got too—too full of—"

" 'Willadean'?" Cade couldn't help himself. The chuckle that escaped spread a smile across his face he couldn't control. This redheaded paragon of control was really named Willadean? There was a chance for her yet.

"Letty, the coffee," Rusty said curtly.

Cade gave Letty a wink and ambled to his feet, following his hostess into the paneled room where he'd found her earlier. The fire had burned down. A grandfather clock outside the door chimed out the hour—seven o'clock. Someone had turned on the lamps, revealing a room that was both masculine and comfortable. In an alcove was an oversize oak desk piled with paperwork. An adjoining wing of the desk housed a small computer and printer.

He lifted an eyebrow. "A computer?"

"I'm determined to make this ranch a modern, efficient operation, McCall. It has to be. Competition is fierce. The odds for success are against us. There is only so much usable water in the state, and there is an ongoing battle over it between the farmers and the ranchers. I have to know where I am and where the ranch stands at any given moment."

"And are you?"

"Am I what?"

"Keeping up with the competition, staying ahead of the odds?"

Rusty couldn't hold back a sigh. "Sometimes. Sometimes not."

"What's the problem?"

"Not that it will make any difference to you, but if you choose to accept my proposal, you're entitled to know. Drought has changed the way we do business. We're fighting against government regulations, manpower shortages, higher prices, and the weather."

"Pretty much the same problems I have as a pipeline troubleshooter—weather, competition, and maintenance—universal enemies of profit and success."

"All of which could change if my new breeding program produces a drought-resistant beef cow, as I expect it to."

"Drought-resistant cows? What are you doing—crossing cows with camels?"

"Almost. As I mentioned when we were flying in, I've bought a new bull, from Africa. He's the first of a new experimental line of cattle that can live on less water for longer periods of time."

"Do you really think it will work?"

"My competition doesn't." *And neither does my banker,* Rusty could have added. She poured the coffee and offered a cup to Cade. "How do you take it?"

"Straight, just like I do my information. When do we get to the why-hire-Cade-McCall answers?"

"All right. I'll try to explain. At least we can get the main issue resolved before we agree on the contract."

"And what is the main issue?"

"The special services I require, Cade."

"I'd be interested in hearing about those. I thought range wars went out with the nineteenth century. I'm not a hired gun. I know nothing about cattle ranching, and I don't have a penny to my name. So what could I possibly have to offer you?"

She took a sip of coffee and looked down at the cup with a frown. "I don't quite know how to begin."

"Start with the ad. I was under the impression that you were simply a widow who needed a hired hand. Then I learn that you want a man you can groom to be a husband. Obviously, now that I've seen you, that isn't the whole truth. You could probably marry any man you wanted. What do you really want from me?"

Rusty fought the low-grade tremor that kept her knees unsteady. She put the cup down on the table and turned her back to the probing eyes of the man standing too close to her. It wasn't too late to back out. She could simply give him a bonus check and say she'd changed her mind. Every sane thought in her mind urged her to do so. Every emotion that she'd kept long submerged surged forward to block out her reservations.

"Children, McCall. After a reasonable period of time, I want you to give me children."

The sip of coffee Cade had just swallowed lodged in his throat somewhere below his vocal cords and around his windpipe. Children? He'd considered that she might want a man, or the "services" of a man, but thoughts like those had vanished the moment he laid eyes on her. This woman could draw men like a honeycomb attracts a hungry bear.

She turned, forcing herself to face him. "Do you understand, McCall? I want children, several children, as quickly as I can produce them."

"Why?" This time there was no disguising the hoarseness in his voice.

"The answer is simple. Silverwild is my life as it was my father's. I will not let it end with my death. I was an only child, and my late husband was incapable of giving me children. I want heirs— legal, legitimate heirs. For that I need a husband."

"Why me?"

"That is a bit more complicated. For reasons that I won't go into, there are no suitable men in the area. I have neither the time nor the inclination to go looking out-of-state. Singles bars and dating services are a waste of time."

"What about artificial insemination? I'd think that a cattle breeder would be more than willing to adopt such a procedure."

"You're right. Normally I would. But artificial insemination is time-consuming, expensive, and not always reliable. Aside from the fact that it would be difficult to keep such a procedure secret. Advertising for a man I could secretly interview as a potential husband seemed the most expedient means of solving the problem."

"Less emotional, less personal than offering yourself to someone you know, I can understand that," he admitted. "By choosing an outsider who's ignorant of the ranching business you can get what you want without losing control. But how can you be sure that I can produce?"

"I'm not. My investigation simply stated that you have already fathered a child, that you're a healthy specimen. You have no bad habits and no ties to any place or anybody. However, because of the variables, I've come up with contingent plans. We sign a preliminary agreement to—work together for six months. If at the end of six months I am not pregnant, you will be given a bonus and a release from the agreement."

"Six months. Not much time to prove myself, is it?"

"I'm thirty-two years old, McCall. I'm the one who doesn't have a lot of time."

"And if you are pregnant in six months, what then?"

"We will marry. On the birth of my child I will give you twenty-five percent of Silverwild. Of course, I will continue to operate the ranch just as I do now. After several children are born, we'll get a quiet divorce, and I'll buy back your stock. You'll be a wealthy man."

"What happens if you're not pregnant?"

"I'll pay you a flat fee of ten thousand dollars for your service and offer you quarters until you can make other arrangements."

"I see." And in some crazy logical way he did. He didn't believe for one minute that she was as unemotional about this undertaking as she was pretending. An unemotional woman would seek out and adopt a healthy child who could be groomed from birth to be the heir. But this woman wanted to bear her own, not one child but several.

And that was how she gave herself away. Her child had to be just that, her flesh and blood. He understood her plan. He didn't understand her need.

Janie had never wanted a child. Perhaps she hadn't known she was pregnant at the time she left him, but all the time Pixie was growing up, she'd never told him about their daughter. He'd always believed that her freedom was more important than a father for their child. Now he wasn't sure.

Cade had seen Janie as a strong woman. He wondered if she'd been ashamed to let him know the truth when she'd gotten sick. Pixie would have been all she had then, and she wouldn't have been able to give her up. So in her shame Janie had kept Pixie's birth a secret. Cade felt he understood Janie better in death than he had in life.

But there seemed to be nothing hidden about Rusty Wilder. Shocking though it might be, she was open with her plan. Now, with the firelight silhouetting her, Rusty waited quietly while he considered what she'd said. She must have expected him to talk dollars and cents, to ask for special concessions, to make demands. He didn't.

He allowed himself to consider her proposal, weighing the pros and cons, trying without success to erase the picture that flooded his mind— the picture of making love to the enticing woman before him.

With the firelight behind her Rusty could see Cade's face clearly. His expression didn't change. The only indication she had of the war waging inside him was the intense look in his eyes. McCall was a realist too. She felt her respect for the man grow. And that wasn't planned either. This was to be a business arrangement, pure and simple.

"And what about Pixie?" he asked in a voice that didn't reveal the extent of his struggle to control his confusion.

"Your daughter?"

"Yes, my daughter. She's already had one mother desert her. I have no intention of going into any relationship that has a built-in escape hatch without also ensuring that every possible means of success is given equal weight."

"That's why we have a six-month trial period."

"And what happens at the end of six months if we don't agree to make the arrangement permanent?"

"Whatever you wish. You can leave, or you may keep the job and one of the tenant houses with no strings attached. I won't expect you to take any interest in my child. No one will ever know what happened."

"No. I can tell you now that I won't agree to that arrangement. I'm learning to be a father to the child I have. But if I should have other children in the future, I intend to be with them. So, if I become a husband again, business arrangement or otherwise, it won't be a temporary arrangement."

"You can't be serious."

"Oh, but I am. And there's another condition to consider, Mrs. Wilder. I'm not an easy man to live with, and from what I've seen, living with you won't be a cakewalk either. Maybe not now, but there may come a time when I'll get married to give my daughter a good life, but I'll never have children with a woman who doesn't want me as much as I want her. If the love isn't there, the sex had better be."

"I don't understand what you're saying, McCall."

"Let's spell it out, Redhead. You know that I fathered a child. What are you offering, on a personal basis? In other words, what assurances can you give me that marriage to you is worth giving up my freedom?"

"I've already told you that once my child is born, I'll make you a partner in Silverwild. You'll have the kind of life you'll never know otherwise."

"It'll be *our* child, Mrs. Wilder, and money isn't what I mean."

He was looking at her with such intensity that she could almost feel his physical reaction. There was a tightening in the corded muscles of his neck. He stepped forward and reached to place the coffee cup and saucer on the rough-hewn cedar mantle above her right shoulder.

She jumped.

As he drew his hand down from the mantle, he grazed her shoulder with his fingertips, sliding them around her upper arm, across her back to clasp her neck. When the other hand moved around her waist, her body gave an involuntary jerk. The fire behind her was nothing to compare with the heat arcing across the scant space now separating them.

"What—what are you doing, McCall?"

"Making my own investigation, Mrs. Wilder. I may not like being forced into marriage, but I'll do it if it's best for my child. But I'm damned well going to have to want the woman. And she's going to want me too. And right now you're going to give me some guarantee that the feeling between us is as strong as I think it is."

"I don't understand." Her voice was a whisper, barely audible above the wild pounding of her heart and the thundering of her pulse.

"No, I don't think you do. But you might as well know, Redhead. I don't come cheap. I don't think your detective's report is quite complete. We both ought to know what we're paying for."

Three

Rusty gasped.

Cade turned her around, bringing her face into the light, drawing her closer until her breasts skimmed his chest. He could feel the beat of her heart and the unevenness of her breathing.

The coals in the rock fireplace became prisms of light reflected in the mirrors of her gown and the turbulence of her green eyes. His fingertips stole through her hair—not coarse as its color might have suggested, but soft, fine as silk. It brushed against his hand like hundreds of tiny jolts of electricity.

With slow caressing motions he trailed her fingertips up her face. He pulled the combs from her hair and watched the long red locks spill across her shoulders.

Rusty's response was intense. She recognized the look of hunger in Cade's eyes. He was staring at her the way the ranch hands stared at the girls in town when they trucked the herd to market. She hadn't understood the raw desire that fed that kind of expression until now—now that she felt it too. Cade McCall had turned her body into hot quicksand with no substance and no form. The feeling was heady. She drew in a deep smoldering breath.

Knowing that she was in danger of losing control of both the situation and her own emotions, Rusty closed her eyes and broke the hot connection between them. No matter how much she might relish the feeling, she couldn't allow this to happen . . . on his terms. It was time she pulled back and made him understand how it would be. She'd never played before. Now she'd try. Tilting her head, she parted her lips hesitantly, moistening them with her tongue.

Cade told himself he hadn't intended to kiss her. But when she leaned into him, a yearning deep inside caught fire, and suddenly he was assaulting her lips, his tongue inside her mouth, his body molding itself to the woman whose very essence had drawn him like a magnet since he'd first seen her in the airport.

She wasn't pulling away. Like a cat, she was making little purring sounds, digging her nails into his back, urging him to greater intensity. Her arms moved up and locked around his neck. Cade felt a tremor sweep through her, rippling up those arms and settling in fingertips that asked for more than he'd expected to give. He slid his hand down the back of the silky dress, past the slick mirrors, feeling the curve of her back and the rounded cushion of her bottom filling his palm as he cupped her boldly to his body.

Cade groaned. The very air he was breathing was blazing. The woman was burning him up.

Suddenly Rusty tore her mouth from his and looked up. Her passion-filled eyes glazed with a confident surge of triumph. "I would say," she whispered throatily, "that I passed your test, McCall. I'd say you want me. What do you think?"

Her arms slid from around his neck, down across his heaving chest, pausing at his belly button, and coming to rest on what best measured his desire.

Rusty knew her face was flushed. Her eyes felt dry, open too wide under his stern gaze. McCall was right about desire. Never in her wildest imagination had she anticipated this response to a man. From the moment she'd laid eyes on Cade McCall, every glance, every word had fanned the flicker of heat that had sprung to life when he'd embraced her.

But the flame had flared out of control when he kissed her. Her simple plan to make him want her had backfired. It was she who wanted him. Dear God, how she wanted him. Through her fumbling adolescent years of rebellion, through eight years of a marriage in name only, she'd never felt one smidgen of the desire Cade McCall's kiss elicited from her.

For a long moment he could only stare at her. Then the beginning of a smile washed across his face, and he let out a long satisfied groan as he nodded. If he'd wondered before whether he was dealing with an angel or a witch, he didn't wonder anymore.

"You're right, Mrs. Wilder, ma'am. I said I'd be damned if I made love to a woman I didn't want. I think that I could also be damned if I do. But there's one thing that a realist like yourself will have to admit. The attraction here is mutual."

Mutual? Try overwhelming, Rusty thought. The feeling wasn't subsiding. Pulling away from his kiss had been nearly impossible for her. She wanted more. Now she tried to cover her restlessness and confusion by moving around Cade to the other side of the desk.

"In the spirit of honesty, McCall, I'll agree that a mating between us won't be unpleasant, but there are other considerations."

"'Mating'?" Cade shuddered. *Mating* was the word for what they were on the verge of. He'd talked about making love, but he'd been wrong. Whatever this was between them was pure animal passion, and he'd been as close to taking her as she'd been to giving herself. But it had been Rusty who'd pulled back, and he was still shaken by the kiss.

"'Other considerations'," he repeated. "I expect so, but at the moment I can't seem to think of any."

Rusty recognized that McCall wasn't having an easier time bringing his physical reactions under control than she was. At least there was no pretense between them. Frankly, she wasn't expecting such honesty from the man. She wasn't accustomed to revealing the truth of her own feelings either. She was out of her depth.

In spite of her bravado Rusty was much too rattled to remain within arm's length of Cade McCall. She'd proved her point, but the interchange had left her stomach churning wildly, her heart skipping, and her pulse plummeting through her veins like hot lava. It suddenly became important that she find a safe place where she could allow her racing heart to settle down. She started toward the door, trying desperately to find a reason for her flight, and caught sight of an open-mouthed Letty standing in the hallway. How long had Letty been there?

Letty's mouth broke into a broad knowing smile. "You folks all right in here? You both look a little—rocky."

Rusty looked imploringly at Cade, then back toward Letty's beaming face.

Cade took a deep breath. "We've just been over some rough road, Letty," he explained with deceptive coolness in his voice. "At the moment we're both suffering from a raging case of frustration."

Rusty spun around. "Stuff it, McCall," she snapped. "There's nothing frustrated about me. If I want something, I go after it."

"Humph!" Letty interjected, "And maybe sometimes you don't know what you want. I'd better tell you, Cade, I didn't approve of Rusty's wild idea to hire herself a husband to begin with. I thought there were plenty of men around here ready and willing. She didn't need to advertise for a yes man." Letty grinned. "Maybe I was wrong. Maybe you're just what she needs."

"Letty." Rusty's voice was full of bristling warning. "I don't *need* a man. If I get one it's purely for business purposes."

"Sure," Letty agreed. "If that's what you want to call it, it's fine with me, but I wonder what your father would say about his daughter contemplating marriage to a hot-blooded—gigolo."

Cade scowled. "I may be hot-blooded, Letty, but I'm no gigolo."

"No, I don't think you are. But you sure aren't what Rusty expected."

"And the widow isn't exactly what I was expecting either, Letty."

Rusty gave an exasperated toss of her head, turned, and headed toward the window. "I'd appreciate it if you two wouldn't talk about me as if I weren't here. I'm trying to conduct a business deal here, Letty."

"Yeah, looked real businesslike, all right," Letty observed mildly.

"It doesn't matter what we—I—you expected," Rusty went on with a frown. "My goal is the same now as it was when I started—a husband and children. Whether or not you, Mr. McCall, have the good sense to accept my offer is yet to be determined."

Cade didn't reply. Instead he stood there, rocking back and forth on the balls of his feet. He wasn't smiling, but Rusty could almost feel his hidden amusement and his growing confidence. She wasn't losing control, but neither was she gaining it. If they'd been playing poker, they'd both have thrown in their hands.

Letty glanced from Cade to Rusty and back again. "How do you feel about changing your name to Wilder after the marriage, Cade?" she asked innocently.

"Now, Letty, love, you know that I have no intention of changing anything, my name or myself. This marriage isn't a done deal yet. In fact, I'm not sure that I'm even interested in this offer."

Rusty looked startled. "And I thought you were a gambler, Mr. McCall. What exactly are you taking a chance on? Wealth? Position? Success?"

"I seem to remember another man who was offered great riches. His name was Faust, and he lost his soul."

A quick fear swept through Rusty. She clenched her fists and stepped toward her mail-order groom. "Let's stop jockeying for position, Mr. McCall. Any permanent arrangement will be based on a written contract that we both agree to. But we're not there yet. We have six months to work out the details. If you have doubts about the trial basis I've suggested, you should take the night to consider my proposal. If my offer of money, a home, and being a mother to your daughter isn't a good enough reward for your services, then so be it. You have a return ticket. Go back to Alaska, and we'll forget we met."

There was a long rigid moment of silence as they stared at each other before Letty's voice cut through the tension. "Stuff and nonsense, Willadean Wilder! If ever two people were a match for each other, you two are. Ahhhh, the children you'll have. And I'm thinking that no piece of paper is going to hold you back, and there's no point in either one of you fooling yourselves."

Rusty gasped. Letty was right. One touch by Cade McCall, and every sane thought about her future had left her mind. Granted, he might be the perfect candidate for fatherhood, but loosing sight of her objectives because of pure lust was foolish.

"McCall, Letty may be right. I'm beginning to think that I may have made a mistake. One of the other applicants might be a better choice. I'm glad you insisted on a . . . demonstration, Mr. McCall—"

"I don't know if we're a 'match,'" Cade said,

cutting her off, "but something happens when we're together, and I don't think you want to end it just like that—without giving it a chance, do you?"

"What do you mean?"

"No point in either of us trying to pretend otherwise. We are volatile together, too volatile to make sense. And this isn't turning out as either of us anticipated. Maybe we'd better sleep on it. Then you can decide what you want, Mrs. Wilder."

What she wanted? That stopped her. McCall was right about their chemistry. What she wanted was to throw herself back into his arms. Rusty studied his stern expression. Oh, yes, she understood the reference he'd made to a man's selling his soul to the devil. She was beginning to understand that she might be in danger of losing hers. She didn't know how to stop it, or even if she wanted to.

"What I want, Cade McCall? I don't know. Suddenly I don't know at all." Garnering every ounce of strength left in her, she straightened her shoulders, turned, and strode from the room. She was halfway up the stairs when she heard his voice in the foyer behind her.

"If it's any consolation to you, Redhead, neither do I."

The sun leaped over the black mountains in the distance and brought with it the harsh light of day. From his window Cade McCall watched the world come to life. In the pastures the cattle appeared to be dirty white rocks being brushed by a sea of brown grass that gently swayed in the crisp air.

He watched below as Rusty strode purposefully

across the distance between the house and one of the barns. From where he stood, he could see a charged smile of anticipation on her face. She pulled herself up on the bottom rail of the fence and shaded her hand with her eyes as she gazed past the front of the house. This morning she wore spring-green-colored corduroy pants under the fleece-lined denim jacket she'd had on the day before. A bright paisley scarf caught her copper hair at the back in a loose knot.

Cade had hoped that a good night's sleep would bring logic to his disordered thoughts. It hadn't. If anything his senses, too, were in greater turmoil. The thrumming in his veins heightened. Just the sight of her proud face brought an unbidden lift to his entire being. And he wanted nothing more than to vault across the banister and join her where she clung to the corral fence.

Eugene had told stories about men who'd gone mad from wilderness fever and married the first woman they met when they reached civilization. But Fairbanks wasn't wilderness, and he had already married once in haste.

He'd gone into marriage with the usual expectations when he'd married Janie. He'd been with the coast guard, away from his home base in South Carolina for the first time, assigned to duty in Washington State. He was lonely and homesick. Then Janie had come along. She was older, a woman looking for a ticket out of a seaport town. And they'd been each other's port in the storm— for a time. He'd given her credit for trying. But the marriage had been a mistake from the first. He'd mistaken sex for love. She'd mistaken a uniform for success and his desire for her as the kind of constant adoration that she craved. But he'd had to be away too much, and Janie needed company. She wasn't too particular, he learned each time he returned.

Four years later he'd come home to an empty house and a note that she was filing for a divorce. She'd found someone would be there for her when she needed him. He hadn't contested her decision. Instead he'd left the coast guard, drifting from one job to another, never allowing any one place or person to pin him down, until he'd finally ended up on the Alaskan pipeline.

It had been four more years before he'd learned that Janie had never followed through with the divorce. She was still his wife. He'd assumed that he'd never gotten any papers because he'd moved around. He might never have known except that Janie was sick and the bill collectors managed to track him down. When Janie's hospital bills came to him, he paid. When Janie died, a stranger delivered his daughter, Jennifer, to him, the child he'd never known.

One look at Pixie's great dark eyes had convinced him without doubt that she was his. Even if she hadn't been, the memory of himself as a rejected eight-year-old boy who was so unhappy that he finally gave up and ran away from home seven years later would have made him accept her.

Neither shy nor frightened, Jennifer had quickly captured the devotion of Eugene, who'd been pressed into service as a nanny. It had taken longer for Jennifer to become "Pixie" and notch out a part of Cade's heart. He'd nearly died along with her when she was so sick. She was already late in starting back to school because of her health and because his camp was too far from town.

Eugene was right. Pixie deserved a different kind of life than in a pipeline camp: a father who was a line troubleshooter and was gone much of the time; a gruff old sourdough as her caretaker. So he'd put his own feelings aside and answered the ad, the ad that brought him to this ranch and a wild, red-haired woman who had offered him a strange proposal of marriage.

If he accepted Rusty's proposal, it would be with his eyes wide open. Whatever attraction he felt to this woman had to be tempered with reality. What was best for Pixie would be the deciding factor, not what he wanted. And getting to know more about his potential employer was the only way he'd be able to determine that.

With that decision made, he pulled on a down vest and loped down the stairs to the kitchen where Letty had a cup of coffee and a sweet roll waiting for him.

"Figured you wouldn't want to sit down and eat either. Rusty's worse than a kid at Christmas, waiting for that bull to be delivered. She's out—"

"At the corral," Cade cut her off. "I saw her from the window."

"I thought you might. Heard you walking around up there."

Cade winced. He'd spent more than a few hours pacing back and forth last night. After bolting his breakfast he went out to the yard.

As he watched Rusty Wilder, his thoughts danced around in his head like the plastic Ping-Pong balls in a bingo machine. She slowly turned her head, finding his gaze and locking onto it with a frown.

"I didn't expect you up so early," she said.

"I might as well have come downstairs two hours ago," he answered, "I couldn't sleep. Change in altitude, I suppose. When's your pretty new boy due?"

"'Pretty boy'?"

"The bull."

"Oh, any minute now."

"How long will it take you to prove your theory about the new crossbreed?"

"I don't know," she admitted, allowing a twinge of doubt to show in her eyes. "Probably too long. If the snowmelt is as light as anticipated, the Silverwild may be in jeopardy before I'm able to produce the kind of cow I'm going for."

"You mean I'm likely to lose my twenty-five percent before I ever get it?"

"Then you've decided to accept my offer?" She forced her voice to remain calm, to conceal the unreasonable spurt of adrenaline that his words inspired. Sometime before dawn she'd decided that a business arrangement with Cade McCall could exist in spite of the tension between them. That would pass, once they'd . . . mated. The excitement now was enhanced because of anticipation, because she'd never had a relationship with a sensual man. It was the end result that she had to consider—children. If their relationship was wildly exciting in the meantime, she wouldn't fight it. From what she'd seen of people and animals, once they'd mated, they lost their craving for each other. Desire served a necessary purpose.

It was temporary and could therefore be dealt with on a logical basis.

Once she'd arrived at her decision, she'd believed that she was prepared for him. She wasn't. Desire was one thing, but when it interfered with the operation of Silverwild, she couldn't allow it. And it just had. She'd already blurted out her fears, and she'd never done that before. She held on to the fence and tried to concentrate on his readiness to answer.

"No, I haven't made a decision yet about the marriage. But if you're pulling a scam about what you're offering me, at least you're the most honest crook I've met. And"—he caught the tie of her scarf and held it for a moment—"the most beautiful too."

"Don't, Cade. I know that I'm not beautiful. You don't have to flatter me. Those kinds of lies aren't part of the deal."

"If a man never told you you're beautiful before— and proved to you he wasn't lying—well, then I guess there are *some* things you're not an expert at. I'm glad. Being close to you is intimidating enough."

"Cade," she whispered, "please don't. I can't seem to think when you're so close."

"I know," he answered. "I'm having some problems with that myself."

"Then don't you think we ought to avoid— touching?"

"Yes, we ought to," he agreed, and draped the scarf along her cheek, letting his fingers touch her for just a moment.

"Look, there's the truck," one of the hands shouted.

Cade dropped the scarf and turned around, his hand resting possessively on Rusty's shoulder as if they had known each other years instead of hours.

A cattle truck was racing along the road toward the barn, throwing a cloud of dust behind it. The driver slowed the truck, came to a stop, and began to back toward the corral. Cade could hear the excited snorting of the new bull inside the trailer. He sounded violent even before the back gate was lowered and the huge red animal charged toward the fenced area.

"He's sure a mean 'un, Rusty," the driver observed as he piled out of the cattle hauler. "Like to butted the back wall of the cab to pieces on the way out here."

The bull charged around the outer fence, then walked slowly to the middle of the corral and pawed at the ground, all the while snorting and bellowing as he glared at the watching group of hands.

The bull had a large chest, a hump on his back the size of a buffalo's, and a lean, hairy rear end. His long tail swished sharply from one side to the other as his huge red-lined eyes darted back and forth. His head was large and flat, and his heavy curved horns extended out at least twelve inches in each direction.

Cade let out a long whistle. "This is a bull from Borneo, Mrs. Wilder. When you go out on a limb, you take a saw with you."

"What do you mean, McCall? He's just what we need. See the hump? That's where he'll store the extra water, in the mound of tissue. So what if he isn't beautiful? We don't care what he looks like. It's the cattle he sires that count."

"Maybe, but if I were one of those cows and saw that hellish-looking creature heading for me, I'd get out of Dodge—quick! How do you expect to control him?"

"That's no problem," she said with more assurance than she felt. "We're accustomed to handling mean bulls. It comes with the territory. Let's get him settled, boys."

But half an hour later all the hands were forced to concede that for now this bull was right where he was going to stay. Rusty gave up and accompanied one of the cowboys to the barn where they'd penned up a cow who was ready to calve. Cade fell in beside her.

Rusty felt his presence, though she didn't comment on it. Instead she continued talking to the man who acted as her foreman. "She's in the barn?"

"Yep. Found her out in the north pasture this morning. I had a feeling she was due, and we loaded her up and brought her in."

"You think she's in trouble again, Doak?"

"I'll be blessed if she ain't. Who'da thought that she'd try to bring another puny calf here backward?"

"After this, get rid of her. She'll never be a good breeder."

"Have you called the vet?" Cade asked.

Rusty cut her eyes at him, chastising him for the interruption. "Vet? Calves coming breech are everyday affairs, McCall. A rancher has to learn to do his own veterinary work if he's to survive."

She moved into the barn, removed her jacket, and hung it on a nail. She rolled up her sleeves and stepped into the stall, standing behind a cow with extended heaving sides. Rusty dunked her right hand and arm into a pale of foul-smelling liquid. "Disinfectant," she said, letting it drip dry as she came up behind the groaning cow, touching her haunches with her left hand and speaking softly.

"What can I do to help?" Cade asked quietly.

Rusty gave a quick glance over her shoulder. "You want to help? Okay. But I give the orders, and you take them. No questions. Understand?"

Cade nodded.

"Fine. Get in the stall and hold her head. Don't let her lie down, and don't let her turn around."

Cade slid by Rusty, taking a cue from her earlier action, sliding his hand up the cow's back and talking quietly to her until he reached the front of the stall where he could catch her halter.

For the next half hour he watched as Rusty inserted her arm into the cow and gradually turned the calf around, an inch at a time, between contractions. He held and handed and followed her directions with no comment. When he was sure that she must be totally exhausted, he heard the weak cry of the calf and Rusty's pleased sigh of relief. The calf's head was showing between Rusty's arms.

"Push, Mama," she coaxed, whispering soft words of encouragement over and over. A human mother couldn't have wished for better care than the cow was being given by Mrs. Rusty Wilder.

There were tears of joy glistening in Rusty's eyes when she held up the calf and walked around to the cow's head. "Here she is, a little girl. She wants her mama."

The exhausted cow turned immediately and began to lick her calf. Above the cow's head, Rusty and Cade's eyes met, and he felt a special warmth, a joining of purpose. They both smiled. In that moment he knew that he'd agree to her proposal. Such a woman was more than the head of Silverwild. She was a woman who had much to give to a child—and a man.

Rusty left the cow and her calf to Doak, washed her hands, paying little attention to her soiled clothing, and slid her arms into the jacket Cade was holding for her. For a moment she leaned against him, and they shared the satisfaction of what they'd accomplished. Then she turned and started back to the house.

"I'll be leaving tonight, Rusty," Cade said simply. "Pixie and I will be back in a few days—if you're still sure about your proposition."

Rusty stopped and turned around. "Are you certain, Cade?"

"No, I've probably never been less certain of a thing in my life. But I'm willing to give it a chance. Six months. Then we'll see. One thing . . ."

"What's that?"

"Pixie and I will stay in one of your tenant houses. I don't want my daughter to be disappointed if this doesn't work. If she sees me as another ranch hand, she won't get her hopes too high."

"No, Cade. If we're going to get to know each other, it has to be on more intimate grounds than that. Letty already has the two rooms in the guest wing ready for you. They were originally built for my grandmother. She wanted her quarters to be private. You work for me. More than that your daughter doesn't need to know."

"I hope this isn't a mistake, Rusty."

Rusty. That was the first time he'd used her name. She felt her heart take a funny little leap. She didn't know what to say. Finally she added, "You know that Letty has her heart set on looking after Pixie. She can't wait either."

"Letty?"

There was a long silence.

"Letty and I," she corrected, and turned back toward the house. This time her practiced long strides were forgotten as she considered the decision they'd just made. She gave way to a more natural rolling walk, the kind of feminine walk that even tired legs couldn't disguise.

Cade felt a tightening in his groin. It was good that he was leaving, that Pixie would soon be here. He wasn't sure how long he'd be able to maintain a safe distance from Rusty. He wasn't sure how long he wanted to.

Business, he reminded himself.

A business relationship.

Except—this business was sex.

He was being hired to do a job, a job for which he appeared to be very well qualified, if his present response to Mrs. Wilder was any guarantee.

Four

Pixie's dark eyes widened as she took in the barren landscape from the backseat of the Jeep where she sat, clutching Eugene's hand. Eugene hadn't been part of the deal with Rusty. But Pixie had wanted Eugene, and he'd surprised Cade by insisting on buying his own ticket. Cade only hoped that Rusty would find something on the ranch to keep the crusty old man busy.

Doak, Rusty's foreman, had been sent to meet their plane and drive them back to the ranch. The drive was long and tiring for a six-year-old making her second move within a year.

"Where's the snow, Daddy?" Pixie asked.

"In the mountains, Pix. They've had a light fall this year."

"Oh," Pixie said in a quiet little voice.

"Where're the trees, Cade?" Eugene asked, disgruntled.

"In the mountains. The Mormons who first came here cleared the land for planting."

"Oh," Eugene said.

"All right, you two. This isn't any easier on me than it is on you. I know that it's different from Alaska, but we agreed that we'd come to Utah and give it a try."

"Maybe, but I thought the 'it' we were trying out was the widow Wilder, and I don't see any sign of her," Eugene grumbled as he tried to fold his long legs into the small space behind the front seat where he'd insisted on loading himself. "Seems to me that she could have found time to meet us personally."

"Rusty would have come," Doak insisted, "except she had a meeting of the state water commission, and she won't be back until tonight. She didn't know when you were coming."

"Trouble?" Cade questioned.

"She didn't say," Doak answered without elaborating.

By the time they reached the ranch, the temperature was beginning to drop, and the sky was swimming in thick gray clouds.

"Looks like there's a storm coming up," Doak observed with a frown. "Hope Rusty gets on in here 'fore it breaks."

Cade didn't have to be told how dangerous it would be for Rusty to land in a snowstorm, particularly in the dark. He didn't comment.

The first big flakes were floating to the ground as the house came into view.

"Daddy, it looks like Zorro's house in the movies. Are there horses?"

"Yes, honey. It's built like a Spanish hacienda,

and there're horses and cows and a few chickens," Cade answered as he began to unload their cases, preoccupied now. Where was Rusty?

"Cade! And this must be Jennifer." Letty came through the doorway, wiping her hands on her apron. "You all come in here quick before you freeze. Who's this?" She turned to Eugene with a critical frown.

"I'm Eugene P. Manderville," the man in question answered testily, adding, "And I'm part of the family."

Letty's only comment was "Humph."

Manderville? Cade bit back a smile. If he'd ever heard Eugene's last name, he'd forgotten it long ago.

Pixie was soon settled at the big oak table in the kitchen, Letty pouring hot chocolate and serving a plate of big chewy cookies. Eugene, on the other side of the table, was eyeing Letty with his best "show me" expression. When she offered him a cup, his eyes widened in disbelief.

"Hell's bells, woman. Is that all you've got to offer a man who's come thousands of miles? I see I'm going to have to introduce you to Tundra Tonic."

"You haven't traveled thousands of miles, Eugene, and it's the middle of the afternoon." Letty dismissed his complaint and filled his cup with chocolate. "What in heaven's name is Tundra Tonic?"

"It's a little something that I bottle myself, good for what ails you."

"I'll bet." Letty rolled her eyes skeptically. "But maybe I do have a little something extra for you."

"Well, I should hope so."

Letty beamed at Eugene and plopped a marsh-mallow into his cup.

Cade shook his head to Letty's offer of hot chocolate. He couldn't be still. He walked to the window and peered into the snow, not yet falling heavily but blowing gracefully across the open ground between the house and the barn. "How's the bull doing?"

"Hard to tell," Letty answered slowly. "Whoever decided to call him Pretty Boy had a real sense of humor."

"'Pretty Boy'?" Cade couldn't hold back a smile. That had been his name for the bull.

"Yep, he ain't pretty, and he has a strange way of picking his ladies."

"Oh, you mean he has to advertise too?" Eugene asked dryly.

"I mean no such thing. I mean he prefers the wild ones on the range to the champions that Rusty offers him. Just like a man. Don't know what's good for him."

Pixie finished her cocoa and began to yawn. "Daddy, I feel sleepy."

"Of course, you are, little one." Eugene started to rise. "And I think I'll join you in taking a nap. I'm a little tuckered out myself. Where's the bunk-house, woman?"

"Eugene, you aren't taking that child out of this house. She has her own room, right next to her daddy. Come along, darling, Letty will show you." She gave Eugene a warning frown and took Pixie's hand. "You, you can find your own bed. The bunkhouse is beyond the barn."

"Now, just a minute," Eugene began.

"Let it be," Cade said, and moved back toward

the window again, satisfied that Pixie was not afraid to go with Letty. "I don't think Letty likes you, Eugene," he observed.

"Well, that's where you're wrong, Cade," Eugene retorted with a chuckle. "She and me, we're going to get along just fine. You wait and see. Think I'll go see if my trunks made it to the bunkhouse. You going to be okay here without me?"

"Yes. I'll be fine."

But he wasn't. There was a gnawing edge of unease in his stomach as the storm worsened. Finally he pulled on a slicker he found hanging by the back door and dashed toward the barn, calling out as he threw open the door, "Doak?"

But Doak didn't answer. The ranch hand pitching hay into one of the stalls looked up in surprise. "Can I help you, sir?"

"How do I get to the hangar, the airfield where Mrs. Wilder will land?"

"Guess you could take the truck."

"Fine. The keys?"

"Inside it."

Cade offered a measured thank-you for the well-traveled road. The snow was beginning to come down now, and in no time it would obscure any landmarks. Suddenly the hangar loomed up before him. Sliding out of the truck, he slammed the door and ran inside.

Standing at the open end was a worried Doak. "Fool woman. She'd have to be crazy to try to land in all this."

"Don't you have any lights?" Cade demanded.

"In a cow pasture?"

"How does she land in weather like this?"

"Normally she doesn't. Normally she'd wait over and fly in when the bad weather passes."

"Why isn't she doing that today?"

"She has some notion that she ought to be here when her . . . guests arrive. She's been fidgety as a moth caught in a spider's web since you left here. Won't let nobody tell her nothing. Guess she was worried you might not come back. But you did. We're hoping that you can talk some sense into her."

"Me? What makes you think I have any influence?"

"Well, she's had on a dress for two nights in a row, and I've never known her to wear one unless she was going in to town. We figure she's practicing for her new man."

"Is that what she told you?"

"Nope, Rusty don't tell nobody nothing. But she don't usually go around naming bulls 'Pretty Boy' and calves 'Darkeyes,' either. I figured she brought you here for a reason, and being a ranch hand ain't it. Wait a minute. Listen!"

They heard it, the drone of an engine. It seemed to be skipping every now and then.

"Something's wrong," said Cade.

"She's up there," Doak said. "I'm going to take the Jeep to the runway approach. Maybe she'll see the lights and follow me in."

"I'll bring the truck too." Cade climbed in, started the engine, and set off across the field, the lights of the truck making watery beams of light through the mixed snow and rain.

At the end of the runway Doak directed the Jeep's lights toward the point at which the plane should drop into view. Cade pulled alongside. After a tense moment they heard the plane, coming closer and closer until suddenly it was just above them, coming in at high speed as it drew closer to the ground.

Doak put the Jeep in reverse and spun around. "She's going too fast."

At that moment they heard the sound of the collision. The plane dipped its right wing into the ground and spun around, crumpling into a corner of the hangar with a crash.

By the time Cade reached the plane, Rusty was sliding to the ground. She swayed slightly and looked around. Cade covered the distance between the Jeep and Rusty in two steps, lifting her into his arms. As he held her, the snow swirled around, catching in her flame-colored hair like decorations on a Christmas tree. Lightning suddenly split the sky behind the house, followed by a clap of thunder.

"I made it," Rusty said dazedly, "So did you."

"Are you hurt?" Cade asked, gazing down at the woman he was holding.

Was she hurt? No. Was she feeling slightly foolish and disoriented? Yes. She blinked as she looked into his frowning eyes.

"No, I don't think so. Looks like the plane is a little worse for wear, though." She felt his arms tighten around her, and a flush of heat rushed to her face. She would have said more, but a knot seemed to be blocking her throat. She'd been afraid he wouldn't come back, that she'd never see him again. But here he was, holding her as if he'd never let go. She wondered for an instant if she was dreaming.

"Next time, stay over." His voice was snappish

and worried. The urge to claim those parted lips was winning. She was blushing, and that knowledge gave him a warm feeling.

Under the intensity of his gaze Rusty shook her head. He was doing it already, giving her orders, and they hadn't been together ten minutes. "I'll stay over if I think it's the thing to do," she snapped, marshaling her defenses. "Put me down, McCall. I can walk."

"If I thought so, I'd have let you."

Cade strode back to the Jeep and motioned to Doak, who nodded and started the Jeep to drive it back to the house. Cade continued to hold her in his lap, burying his chin in her hair. She was still, too still. Then she began to shiver. When the Jeep stopped, he strode through Letty's empty kitchen, up the stairs, and into the family wing.

"Which room?"

"First door on the right," she managed to say.

She should be struggling, opposing his take-charge attitude. Instead, her arms had found their way around his neck, and her fingertips were playing on the skin beneath the collar of the slicker. She liked the way his hair curled against his collar. She liked the way it felt, the way he smelled. She tried to pull herself together. "Where's—your daughter?" she managed to ask.

"My daughter is where you're about to me—in bed."

"Bed? Why?"

"For a rest. She's had a long trip."

He tightened his grip for a moment, feeling the touch of her breast against his chest, the little warm breaths of air against his neck. Then, reluctantly, he let Rusty down and flicked on the lamp beside her bed. "Take off those wet clothes."

Take off her clothes? His words rattled around in her conscious mind until she could focus on the meaning. Rusty shook her head. This time he'd gone too far. Concern for her after she wrecked the plane was understandable, but ordering her to undress? She didn't want to undress. A moment ago she'd been warm. Now she was cold, cold because he wasn't holding her any longer. She felt like a television screen, fading from color to black and white, and back to color again.

Losing contact with his body gave her a respite from the barrage of emotions plummeting her body. She took a deep sensible breath. "Listen, McCall, I won't be dictated to. This is *my* room, and these are *my* clothes. I'll take them off when I'm ready."

"Not this time, Redhead. You've had a shock, and you're wet and cold. This time you take them off when I'm ready. Either you do it, or I'll do it for you."

Shock? Yes. Emotional shock as a result of severe mental pressure. That must explain the strange sensations she was feeling. Her legs felt weak, her thoughts fuzzy. She couldn't even lift her arms to unzip her parka.

Across the room Cade slid out of the damp slicker and let it fall to the floor. He looked around, spotted the bathroom door, and turned on the shower inside. Back at the bed he lifted Rusty and carried her into the bathroom, already filled with steam.

Before she could protest what was happening,

Cade had stripped off her jacket and shirt and was sliding her jeans down her legs.

"McCall? This wasn't part of our agreement."

"We haven't signed an agreement yet, Redhead, and you don't know what terms I may insist on. I have to do something to earn my keep. I'm no cowboy, you know. I think, however, that I could be a very good lady's maid."

"I don't think that you have any experience at that either," she said dreamily. "But you can learn."

Maybe, but first Cade would have to learn control. As Rusty's body came into view, he felt his insides contract. Her breasts spilled over the edge of a lacy red bra that had to have been designed to drive a man wild. The matching panties were heart-stopping. The lingerie looked new. He smiled. He liked a woman who wore silk beneath denim, especially when its color was hot red.

Cade swallowed hard and picked Rusty up, placing her inside the shower stall.

"Oh, no, McCall. If I have to get wet, so do you." With an attempt at being stern, Rusty reached out and jerked a surprised Cade under the spray.

"Listen, you," he began, "you're wetting my boots, and I just bought them."

"Oh? You bought a pair of boots?" She looked down at the shower floor. "So you did. You didn't have to do that. I guess I ought to tell you as my husband-to-be that I intend to keep you barefoot and—no, that's how you keep a woman, isn't it? Well, no matter, we'll improvise."

Her improvising was reaching mercurial heights when Cade became aware of a pounding on the bathroom door.

' "Are you in there, Rusty Wilder?" Letty's voice was marine drill-sergeant intense.

"Of course," Rusty said with a lilt in her voice. "Cade's taking off my clothes."

The door burst open. "He's what?"

"I was trying to warm her up," Cade explained. "She crashed the plane into the hangar, and I think she may be suffering from shock."

"Nonsense, McCall. I'm suffering from frustration, and I'm doing something about it."

"Not today you aren't," Letty said forcefully, giving Cade a jerk of her head that indicated he should vamoose.

"I think I'll let you take over, Letty," he agreed, and backed out of the bathroom before Rusty completely overpowered him. "Ah, Letty, where is my room?"

"Same place as this one, on the other wing of the house," she answered. "And I'm thinking it's a good thing. Out of here, now, before I decide to take off your clothes and turn the cold water on you full blast."

"Yes, ma'am."

"Red underwear!" she was grumbling in mock dismay. "Never worn red underwear in your life. What else did you do to get ready for a husband while you were in Salt Lake City, Willadean Wilder?"

Cade closed the bedroom door, a big foolish grin slashing his face. Sloshing down the hall, Cade decided that a cold shower wasn't a bad idea. But he might want to wait for a while. Right now, all Letty would get if she doused him was steam.

Rusty opened her eyes, glanced over at the clock, and groaned. The sun was streaming through the window. It took her a moment to realize where she was: In bed, covered with two quilts and a spread.

She groaned.

Surely she'd been dreaming. Surely she wasn't remembering what had happened.

Everything from the night before had a surrealistic quality about it. Before she'd left Salt Lake City, she'd gone shopping for underwear—red, feminine underwear. She'd smoked her first and only cigarette. She'd even marched into the airport bar and ordered a Scotch and water. Then she'd flown home through the beginning of a storm and crashed the plane. Worse than that, she had more than a vague recollection that she'd made a fool out of herself with Cade. How could she ever face him?

"Hi. Are you going to be my new mommy?"

Rusty followed the sound of the voice until she found its source—a child, a dark-eyed child with masses of jet-black curly hair and a mouth that seemed to ask a permanent question.

"What?"

Rusty knew what the child had said. At least she thought she did. It was just that she and Cade had agreed that his daughter wouldn't know about their plans. He didn't want Pixie disappointed, he'd said.

"You look like Glenda, the good witch," Pixie said solemnly. "I like Glenda. I like Dorothy too. Do you?"

"Oz! That's where I am," Rusty declared. "I took off from the Salt Lake City airport and landed, not in Kansas, but Oz. All I need is—"

"Pixie? Are you in here?"

"—the Scarecrow."

The man sticking his long neck through the door qualified in every sense of the word. All he needed were strands of hay sticking out from beneath his neckline and his hat.

"Oh no," Pixie said, climbing up on the side of Rusty's bed. "That's not the Scarecrow, that's Eugene. He's my friend. He's probably brought you some Tundra Tonic. He makes it, you know, and it's very good for what ails you."

Rusty closed her eyes.

When she opened them, the door was wide open, and Letty was standing there, glaring at both the child and the odd-looking man. "And I'm the wicked Witch of the West," she said with a snort. "If you two don't get down to breakfast, I'm going to put a spell on you."

Pixie giggled and slid down from the bed. She started toward the door, ran back, and gave Rusty a quick kiss on her cheek. "I think I'm going to like living in Oz. Thank you for hiring my daddy."

"Pixie," Rusty called out, pushing herself to a sitting position. "Who told you that I was going to be your mommy?"

"Oh, I heard Mr. Doak and another man down at the barn talking when I went down to see the bull. I like Pretty Boy too. He's nice. He got very mad when my daddy made me leave."

"So much for secrets," Letty observed with an I-told-you-so click of her teeth as Pixie danced out the door. "Though I don't know why I should expect the hands to keep their mouths shut when you two are up here in the shower taking off each other's clothes as openly as a bare-bottomed lady at the Coyote Springs Saloon."

"Then it's true? Cade did carry me up here and—and put me in the shower?"

"Who knows? When I came in, you were both in the stall, and you were tearing at his clothes. It was not exactly—" Letty sighed dramatically— "ladylike behavior. Though if I were twenty-five years younger, I might wrestle you for him."

Rusty threw her feet over the side of the bed and stood up. It was obvious that Cade had been right. She'd suffered a mild case of shock that had made her behave . . . strangely. Surely Cade understood that, even if Letty was having great fun with what had happened.

"Letty," she began, "I thought that I explained to you what my plans for Mr. McCall are. He's on a trial basis here. If at the end of six months I am—" she blushed, and forced herself to go on, "pregnant, we will get married."

"Humph! Trial for what?"

Rusty swayed for a moment, feeling an unexpected light-headedness. Shock might have been a reasonable excuse for her behavior last night, but even she had difficulty making any such claims this morning. She squared her shoulders, glanced at the clock on her nightstand. "Ten o'clock! Why didn't you call me earlier?"

"Well, after all the excitement, Cade said to let you sleep."

"Cade doesn't make the decisions around here."

"Oh? Try telling the hands that."

Rusty came to an abrupt stop and whirled around. "What do you mean by that?"

"Your bull broke out of the pasture about an hour ago, and Cade's organized a roundup."

"A roundup? I didn't know Cade even knew how to ride."

"Can't say," Letty mumbled airily. "But I guess your trial period will tell you lots of—things. Coffee's on the stove."

"Ohhhhh!" Rusty groaned. She dressed quickly, brushed her teeth, and ran a comb through her hair. "Organized a roundup. Ohhhhh!" What would an oil field drifter know about rounding up a bull? Why would Doak allow him to assume the responsibility anyway? Doak was the foreman. Well, he wasn't exactly the foreman. She had never bestowed the official title on him. She could never bring herself to go that far. It was one of the ways she made certain that she maintained authority. But Cade?

Before Letty got down the stairs and poured the coffee, Rusty was charging out the back door. At the barn the men were already mounted and gathered around Cade, who was standing in the Jeep.

"You know the land," he was saying.

Rusty pushed through the riders. "What's going on?"

"Good morning, Mrs. Wilder." Cade gave her a quick smile, then replaced it with a serious expression and a businesslike nod. "We're about ready to go here."

"Why didn't you let me know what happened?"

"Because we don't know what happened. Only Pretty Boy can tell us when we find him, and we need to get to it before he gets any farther away. Doak, I'll let you give the boys their directions."

Cade stepped down and held out his hand to Rusty, who found herself offering her own before she realized that she was following his orders too. "But—" she started.

"No!" Cade said under his breath, and shook his head.

After a brief moment of surprise Doak cleared his throat and began assigning sections of land for each group to cover. "If you find him, fire two shots, wait, and fire two more. If there is a problem, fire rapidly in bursts. The truck will get as close to you as possible. Understood?"

The men nodded, glanced back at Rusty, and began to disperse. Rusty, unable to hold her tongue any longer, turned to Cade.

"How dare you make decisions around here! You have no right. No right to stop me either, McCall!"

Cade sat down and started the engine on the Jeep. "Sit down, Willadean."

"Don't call me that! And I won't sit if I don't want to."

"Suit yourself." He put the Jeep in gear and gave it gas, biting back the ripple of a smile in the corners of his mouth when Rusty fell back with a jolt. "Why don't you have two-way radios, at least for Doak and yourself?"

"Because—because we don't need them."

"You don't?"

"Well, we never have before. Where are we going?"

"To find your bull."

"What makes you think you know where he is?"

Cade drove rapidly across the pasture and up the slope of the ridge that curved around the lower bottleneck of land through which her plane had dropped the night before. Rusty closed her eyes and winced as they passed the plane, its wing digging in the ground, its tail wedged into the side of the hangar wall.

"I don't know where he is, but I thought we'd find the highest spot around and wait."

"I can't sit here and wait while my men look."

"Why not? Don't you have good men?"

"Yes, of course."

"And isn't Doak your right-hand man?"

"Yes, but—"

"But the bottom line is that you don't really trust him, or is it that you're afraid to delegate authority on the chance that your hands can perform their jobs without you looking over their shoulders?"

Cade drove the Jeep as far up the ridge as he could and brought it to a stop. He didn't know why he was being so hard on her except that he'd been worried that she'd decided to lead the hands.

Turning, he allowed himself to take a long look at Rusty Wilder. He'd thought his memory had played tricks on him last night. She couldn't possibly be as beautiful and as full of fire as he'd thought. But she was. When her plane had slammed into the hangar, he'd felt something deep inside tear, and he'd lost control.

The men he'd worked with had called him distant. But he'd known the truth. He was frozen inside. As long as he refused to allow any emotion to touch him, the wall of ice he'd created remained intact. First Pixie had come and begun chipping away at it, and then last night Rusty had put a big crack in it, so much so that the feared melting had begun in earnest.

Cade felt like the little Dutch boy with his thumb in the hole in the dike, and every time he looked at Rusty another hole appeared. If Letty hadn't interrupted, he'd have taken Rusty to bed and made love to her all night long. There was no doubt about that. And she would have let him. He couldn't have been wrong about her response. She'd been as caught up in desire as he. Had his explanation been right? Had she been suffering from shock? That was likely. And that was the trouble.

For most of the night he'd wrestled with the problem. Why was he having qualms about what had almost happened? If the goal of his being with Rusty was to produce a child, why would making love to her have been wrong? She wanted him; he had no doubt of that. He wanted her. Even now his body reminded him of that fact. Then why?

He didn't know, and that was what was bothering him. So far he'd spent two nights on Silverwild, and he hadn't slept for more than a few hours all told. Sooner or later he'd have to find an answer.

The sun was bright and warm this morning. In the distance the fresh snow on the Wasatch Mountain range glistened. Rusty couldn't look at Cade. She focused her gaze on the snow. If only there were more snow, so many of her problems would be solved.

At least that's what she would have said last week.

Now Cade McCall had just forced her to look at another problem, one he was creating with his interference. Of course she should be out there with her men. They expected her there. They were a team. She'd always directed them. They'd never given her any back talk about her orders. They simply followed them, silently, without comment.

Still, she couldn't help but think about the moment back there when Doak had been handing out assignments. The men had talked to him, verified, asked questions. They never did that with her. But that didn't mean anything. They were just making certain they understood what he'd told them. Cade's implication that she didn't trust Doak had been an unnecessary dig. Doak knew she had confidence in him.

"Of course I trust Doak," she said into the long silence.

"But you don't let him make decisions."

"What business is that of yours, McCall?"

"None, now, but what happens when you're carrying our child?"

Rusty let out a surprised breath as she unclenched the hand that was holding on to the door of the Jeep. "I'll cross that bridge when I come to it."

"Maybe" was his only comment.

"Damn you, Cade McCall," she finally said. "You've only just come here, and already you're trying to do the very thing I explicitly warned you against."

"What's that?"

"Take over Silverwild. *I* am in charge, and I'll stay in charge."

"I know," he admitted, and after a long while turned toward her with genuine regret in his eyes. "You're right, and I'm sorry."

"You are?" An apology was totally unexpected. He was still looking at her with regret. This morning his dark eyes seemed old, very old, as if he'd witnessed the passage of a thousand years and stored those visions somewhere deep inside. There was pain there, and maybe acceptance. She felt her heart pounding and caught her breath. The silence magnified its beat until it seemed to reverberate across the hills and slam against her like the beat of ancient drums.

"You know that I wanted to make love to you last night so badly it hurt. I would have if Letty hadn't come," he said.

"I know."

She was finding it hard to talk. The focus had changed from what was happening now to what had happened last night. She'd known from the first time their eyes met this morning that it was still between them, as strong as it had been then.

"And it would have been wrong," he said.

"Why? That's what you were hired for."

"I know." He broke their eye contact and got out of the Jeep.

She watched him for a moment as he walked up the hill, then scrambled after him, reaching him as he came to a stop at the top of the rise.

"Silverwild is very beautiful. I can understand why you want it to go on forever."

"Then why was it wrong?" Rusty asked again, deliberately looking out across the range, forcing herself to close out the overwhelming physical compulsion she experienced every time they came together. "I wanted you, McCall, and it had nothing to do with the accident. That's something new for me."

"I thought it might be."

"Cade."

This time they turned at the same time. Rusty met his stare and held it defiantly. She didn't know where they were heading, but she knew that he was her answer, her question, and her resolution. She wouldn't allow him to back away.

"Are you sure you want me to stay? You can still change your mind." His eyes went even darker as he asked the question.

Rusty nodded. She brought her hand to his chin and rubbed her fingertips along the rough stubble of his beard. She felt a strange lightness, as if the height on the mountainside might be affecting her balance. A gust of cold air caught at her hair and billowed it behind her.

Cade waited, willing himself not to move.

Rusty's fingers slid down his cheek, around his chin, and rimmed his lips. She marveled at the weathered look of the man. He was like stone—immobile, tense. She had the feeling that if he ever let go, she'd be caught up in the fury of his release like a prairie fire fanned by a crosswind. Down his chin, under his neck to the opening of his shirt her fingertips moved slowly, as if she were measuring the strength of his will.

Heat, more heat, boiling heat was flowing across every nerve ending of her body. Lust, desire, the kind she'd never known before. She knew only that she was on fire and that the man she was touching was chiseled ice beneath her touch. She shivered.

Cade felt Rusty's shiver. His body was wired, his control stretched to the breaking point. The sunlight danced about her hair, fanning little points of light into a blazing fire that licked at every part of his mind. Her touch was light, but he knew that he was lost. He had been from the first moment he'd seen her in the airport.

This kind of instant desire didn't happen. If it

did, it flared up and burned itself out. This intense feeling couldn't survive the heat of its passion. But his desire intensified with every touch. He was like the atomic reactor without the cool-down tank, and sooner or later he would explode.

What was holding him back?

"What are you afraid of, McCall?"

"You, myself, us."

He couldn't take his eyes off her. He watched as her breathing quickened, her lips trembled, her eyes widened.

"Don't do this, Rusty. Not unless you want me to lose all my control."

"Why should I spare you? I've already lost mine."

Abruptly he reached out, slid his thigh between her legs, and jerked her forward as he crushed her lips savagely beneath his. The intimacy was overwhelming. She felt him harden against her leg. He was clasping her against him, arching her body into his as he shattered her with the power of his desire.

A riot of sensation exploded through her body and into every part of her. He was claiming all, and she was giving all. Cade McCall was the master—her master. That knowledge shot through her like the sound of a bullet. She felt her body lurch. Bullet—bullets? What she was hearing was gunshots.

"McCall, stop!"

Cade drew back. "What's wrong? Isn't that what you wanted?"

Rusty drew a deep breath and slid back, separating her protesting body from Cade. "Listen, Cade, the shots. They've found Pretty Boy." She turned away, still breathing hard, and stumbled to the Jeep. "We have to go. You drive, please. I don't think I can."

Cade closed his eyes and tried to regain control. The devil. He was sure his first suspicions were right. Rusty Wilder was a messenger from Satan, and she'd already claimed his soul. As he moved back to the Jeep and started the engine, he desperately tried to remember what happened to Faust.

In the end it didn't matter. He'd already been branded by her flame.

Five

By the time Rusty and Cade reached the entrance to the canyon where Pretty Boy was found, the rest of the men were already there, including Eugene, who was sitting on the fender of the truck.

"How'd you get here so fast, Eugene?" Cade asked gruffly. "You don't know anything about finding stray bulls."

Eugene looked from Cade to Rusty and back again.

"Well, I may not know anything about cattle, but there was this old bull moose once who stayed around the camp so he could mooch off the guys. He was always after the ladies, but he liked to eat good too. Some of us got up a betting pool once on how many ladies he had and how he managed to keep 'em close by. 'Course, if we was going to find out who won, we had to keep a count."

Rusty opened the door and shaded her eyes from the sun. Pretty Boy was somewhere up ahead, but because of the narrow entrance to the canyon she couldn't see him.

"What happened to the moose?" asked one of the hands.

"He found himself a blind canyon just like this and set up moose camp. I figured if it was good for the moose, it ought to be good for a bull. Letty told me where this canyon was. Looks like he's got a couple of lady friends in there," Eugene observed from where he was sitting.

"What do you think, Cade?" Doak rode over to the Jeep.

Rusty was out of the Jeep before Cade could answer. She strode angrily over to one of the hands. "Give me your horse, Joe. You fellows make a tunnel. Doak and I'll go in and drive the bull out. You keep him heading toward the ranch."

Doak looked first at Rusty, then at Cade, a shade of regret coloring Doak's expression for an instant.

Cade watched Rusty as she anxiously waited. He nodded. She was right. Silverwild was hers, and she had the right to make the calls. He'd been wrong to try to move in on her power, even if it had been for her own good to rest after the accident. That had nothing to do with it. He had done what he was accustomed to doing—took charge—and the men had seemed willing to listen to him.

He watched as Doak and Rusty rode into the canyon and the men complied with Rusty's directions, then he walked over to the truck.

"Moose camp, Eugene?"

"Well, it looked like things between you and Mrs. Wilder were a little heated. A good yarn always cools things off. Worked right well, didn't it? At least the hands are cool. You still look a little frazzled. Trouble in paradise?"

"More than a little," Cade admitted. "I think I may have made a wrong move coming here."

"You mean with the future Mrs. McCall?"

"That's exactly what I mean. This was supposed to be a business arrangement, Eugene. I could have handled that. It seems to have changed, and I'm not sure about what's happening."

"Oh, I think you are, Cade. I've always thought that somewhere along the line you lost your sense of direction. You've been up in the ice and snow country so long, you've turned into an iceman yourself. Now you've fallen into the fire, and you're beginning to melt."

"What can I do about it?"

"As I see it, old friend, not a damned thing, except make sure you don't drown in the thaw."

At that moment Rusty and Doak rode back toward the truck. Rusty was red-faced and visibly upset.

"Something wrong?" Eugene asked curiously, as if he had expected her frustration.

"Wrong?" Rusty swore, and flicked the reins of the horse against her thigh. "That bull isn't about to let us drive him anywhere. He's too—too excited. We'll just have to wait until he's . . . done."

Rusty could barely contain her fury. First her emotions had been stroked to the bursting point by McCall's kisses. Then she'd ridden into a blind canyon for a bull who was aroused beyond anything she'd ever witnessed in all her years of breeding cows. Pretty Boy was awesome. He was ready to do his job, and he had no intention of allowing anybody or anything to separate him from the willing cows he'd gathered in the canyon.

The sheer animal instinct of his purpose had fanned her already volcanic emotions to a near explosion. For ten years she'd ridden out with her men without ever feeling the least bit self-conscious about the breeding of the cattle—until today. She looked at the knowing smile on Cade's face and cut the horse around, riding away from the men until she could bring her feelings under control.

"Say Pretty Boy's hot and bothered?" Eugene slid down from the fender and spit a pool of tobacco on the hard ground.

Doak nodded. "They get that way, but this old boy's a real sight. Maybe if he knew us better, we'd get around him. As it is, without a tranquilizer gun I don't think we're going to get anywhere."

Cade looked up. "Tranquilizer gun? Don't you have one?"

"Yep, but Rusty don't like to use it. It isn't as reliable as you think. If you get the dosage too heavy, you can kill the animal. If it isn't heavy enough, you just make him crazy, and then you can't get the antidote into him to bring him out of it. Of course, you can hit the wrong place and kill him with the dart."

"So," Cade asked, "what do we do?"

"We could wait until the fool wears himself out, which, from the looks of things could be days."

"I don't want to do that," Rusty interrupted as she walked her horse slowly back toward the group. "He could injure himself. But at the moment I don't know what else to do. We'll make camp and wait."

"Suppose it's dark by then?" Eugene asked with

a curious expression on his face. Cade knew that meant Eugene was working on an idea, though Cade couldn't imagine what kind of moose story would help now.

"Well, that would make it harder," Rusty admitted. "He could slip by us and reach the open range."

"Do you have an idea, Eugene?" Cade looked at his old friend and waited.

"Maybe. Can I borrow one of these fellows to go back to the bunkhouse with me?"

"Certainly. Go with him, Joe," Rusty said, "but I can't imagine what you have in mind."

"Just a thought, but it might work. Come on, boy." Eugene crawled back into the truck and sent it in a wild circle.

"Are you sure he was the camp cook?" Rusty asked suspiciously.

"Well, 'cook' doesn't quite cover it. Eugene cooked. He also meddled in everybody's business, made things work when they gave out, and generally considered himself the camp den mother."

Rusty made certain she kept Doak between herself and Cade as they waited, but even from a distance she was highly aware of the banked fire in Cade's eyes. She didn't know what might have happened on the mountain ridge if shots hadn't sounded. But she decided that the time had come to make a decision about the preliminary contract before she lost all control of whatever future they might have together.

The phrase "make love" had taken on an entirely different meaning for her now. Every time she was within ten feet of Cade McCall, she became a radio antenna. Her body sent out ready signals and she received a confirmation that was so powerful she could almost feel their electrical connection.

Everything would be better once she got the rules down on paper, she assured herself. Cade would be forced to follow those rules. There would be no more encroaching on her rightful authority. She'd make certain that there was no more letting down, no more giving in, until she was ready. Until—

Until the time was right.

In the canyon she heard the high-pitched lowing of a cow, followed by the sound of hooves plowing the hard ground and the guttural bellow of the bull.

Rusty let out a deep breath and heard a low groan, totally unaware until she caught the look on Doak's face that she'd been the one to make that sound.

It was noon by the time Eugene got back. Curious, the men gathered around, watching as he gathered up a large tin tub and an odd assortment of water buckets and brown long-necked bottles.

"What are you up to?" Doak asked, scratching his chin.

"Well, that old boy sure ain't gonna stop to eat, but that's plenty hot work in there. Just maybe he'll stop to take a drink, wet his whistle now and then. I'm going to give him something that will change his tune."

Inside the canyon Eugene found a level spot beneath an overhang and stationed his tub. He proceeded to fill it with water from the buckets. He opened one of the bottles, took a deep sniff, and turned it up. After taking a long drink, he emptied it and another bottle into the water and stirred the mixture with a wooden stick.

"That ought to do it. Let's pull back and find us a warm spot to wait."

By this time Cade had figured out what Eugene was up to. He wasn't certain it would work, but watching the show would at least relieve the tension between the men and Rusty and Rusty and himself, and if he was right, they'd be entertained at the same time.

"What's wrong with the ladies Pretty Boy picked out?" Eugene asked curiously.

"They're strays, not the caliber of cow that we want to use to prove my theory," Rusty answered. "I plan to use only pure Charbray until we get a good sample of stock."

She climbed down from her horse and sat down on a rock along the canyon wall. "Are you sure whatever you're doing is safe? That bull is the most expensive thing on this ranch. I wouldn't want to take a chance of losing him."

"Absolutely," Eugene guaranteed. "Believe I'll take me a little nap. There's food in the truck if anybody's hungry." With that, he leaned back into a crevice, using a section of rock as protection from the wind.

Doak and the other men moved over to the truck and claimed sandwich bags and thermoses of coffee, leaving Cade and Rusty sitting together, and Eugene off to the side. After a few minutes Cade followed suit, picked up two more thermoses of coffee, and brought them back to share with Rusty, dropping down beside her.

"Tell me about your wife," Rusty asked as she sipped the hot coffee. "Why didn't she tell you about your child?"

Cade looked startled. He thought about her question for a moment, then tried to reason out an answer that made some kind of sense. "Janie was afraid to be alone. She wanted someone to be there for her. I was gone for long periods of time. I think Pixie filled that need for her and she didn't want to take the chance I'd take Pixie away."

"And would you?"

"I don't know. She left me for another man. When he left her, she started to drink. From what I've learned about her condition, I could have won custody of Pixie in court."

From where they were sitting they couldn't see the bull and his harem. It was just as well. Listening to their sounds was bad enough. It wasn't long before Pretty Boy plodded into sight, stopped, sniffed, and found the tub. After a long drink he moved back into the canyon.

"What about your husband?" Cade asked.

"Ben? Funny, I don't think of him as my husband, though he was for eight years. He was my father's partner. Ben was so much older. Growing up, I knew him more as a second father."

"Didn't that make it a bit uncomfortable—trying to be his wife, I mean?"

"Yes." She could have told him that after a few unsuccessful attempts there had been no lovemaking. In the beginning Ben had felt as awkward about it as she had. Then, after his heart trouble began, there'd been no further effort.

"Did you love her?" asked Rusty.

"Janie? I thought so at the time. Who knows? Love is hard to define, I think."

"I never loved Ben," she admitted, "not in the way a woman should love a man. I . . . know that now."

Cade and Rusty didn't look at each other. Their voices were low and unemotional. With the men nearby they simply talked, exchanging information with surprisingly little restraint. Being able to talk like this to a woman was something Cade hadn't experienced before. He thought that Rusty, too, was surprised by their ease with each other.

By the time Pretty Boy made his second trip to the water tub, his stride was unsteady, and his head bobbled. His bellowing took on a distinctly happy sound, and before long he'd deserted the ladies entirely and was concentrating on the tub.

Rusty sat up and looked from the bull to Eugene and back again. "What exactly did you put in that water?"

"My own secret formula," he confessed matter-of-factly. "The boys back at the camp in Alaska called it Tundra Tonic. It's good for what ails you," he said, glancing at Cade.

He ambled to his feet and started back to the truck. "I'd say that your bull won't give you any trouble now. Just lasso one of them ladies and bring her along for company, and he'll be as happy as an old rooster in the henhouse."

"'Tundra Tonic'?" Rusty questioned.

"'Good for what ails you'?" Doak repeated, the beginning of a smile on his face. "Let's go, boys. We'd better get that bull back home before his dose of tonic wears off."

"Ma'am." Joe, the hand who'd gone with Eugene, stood on the ground, shuffling his feet. "Are you done with my horse?"

"Ride with me, Joe," Cade suggested. "That is, if Mrs. Wilder doesn't mind? I'm sure she wants to oversee Pretty Boy's return."

"Uh, no, Joe. I'll let you have your horse back," Rusty said easily. "Doak doesn't need me to ride with him."

She got into the Jeep and slammed the door. "I've been doing some thinking. I'll make arrangements for Pixie to start school in Coyote Wells on Monday. I'll also ask Judge Meekins to come over tomorrow night to draw up our preliminary contract, and—" she caught her breath before finishing in a rush, "there's the Cattleman's Ball next Friday night, which I'll expect you to attend as my . . . escort. If you agree."

She didn't look at him. But he knew that she was giving him one last chance to change his mind. After he agreed, he was committed to—well, he didn't know what exactly. To be a husband? To be a father? He'd been here two days, and he already knew that the trial period wasn't a good idea. Six months would never be enough.

But six months was a start.

"Yes."

Pixie met them at the corral. With a cry of pleasure she slid under the fence and ran toward the bull.

"Oh, Pretty Boy, you're back!"

Rusty felt her heart turn over. "Cade—look out, Pixie!"

Doak, Eugene, and Cade all made a mad dash for the corral, arriving at the same time.

Pixie, singing "Mary Had a Little Lamb," was standing beside the huge bull, who was lowering his head for Pixie to pat him. The sound the bull was making wasn't angry until he raised his head and caught sight of the men pressing toward him.

"Pixie," Cade said in a calm voice, "back away, slowly, now."

"But, Daddy," Pixie argued, "Pretty Boy likes for me to pet him."

"Please, Pix, do as I say."

Pretty Boy was standing very still, his feet planted apart, eyeing the men nervously.

"All right," Pixie agreed. "I'll come back and play with you tomorrow, Pretty Boy."

The bull lowered his head for one last pat and watched as Pixie ran back across the corral and under the fence to be swept up in Cade's arms.

The thundering behind them was the sound of the men trying to reach the safety of the fence before the bull made contact with his horns, lowered and extended.

"I'm glad you found him, Daddy. I don't think he likes being by himself. I think that's why he ran away."

"Pixie, don't you ever get into the pen with that bull again, hear me?" Cade said, his voice still taut with strain. "He could hurt you."

"No he won't, Daddy. He let me pet him this morning. He likes to have his head scratched. I gave him my piece of toast. He likes toast with jelly."

Over Pixie's head Cade caught sight of Eugene, who was nodding in agreement. "She's right,

Cade. I wouldn't have believed it myself if I hadn't seen it. She stood there singing 'Mary Had a Little Lamb.' Then before I realized what she was doing, she was inside that fence, feeding him toast and jelly. And, believe it or not, he liked it."

Cade felt a lump in his throat. Pixie, who'd survived her mother's death and two bouts of bronchitis and pneumonia, had casually stepped into the corral with a wild bull and escaped harm. He hugged her even tighter.

Rusty walked over and slid her arm around Pixie too. "But, Pixie, sweetheart, I think you ought to wait until Pretty Boy is settled in before you start to play with him. Sometimes wild animals like to pretend that they like you when they don't. Do you know the story of Little Red Riding Hood and the wolf?"

"Yes, ma'am. Eugene told it to me."

"You remember that the wolf pretended he was the grandmother so that he could eat up the little girl? Promise me you'll wait until we're sure that Pretty Boy isn't doing that."

"Oh, but he isn't. I know he isn't. But—" she turned her great dark eyes toward Rusty and stopped, "but if you say so, I won't go back into the pen again until you tell me I can."

"I think that would be best for now, Pixie," Rusty answered. "Not every little girl would worry about a bull being lonely. I think you must be very special." Rusty realized with surprise that she really meant what she'd said. She took Pixie's hand as they walked to the house. Cade held his daughter's other hand. As naturally as if they'd always done so, Cade and Rusty, with Pixie between them, made their way into the house.

Letty watched, a broad smile on her face. Maybe Rusty's plan to find herself a mail-order husband was going to work out fine. Maybe she'd just make up that extra room beside hers for Pixie. That child might need comforting during the night until she felt at home on Silverwild.

And, Letty decided airily, you never knew where Cade might be. The two wings of the house were pretty far apart, even if they were connected by the hallway on the inside and the veranda on the outside. Yep, Pixie might like the little room next to Letty's. She could still claim her regular bedroom during the daytime. Letty didn't expect that daytime would be a problem. But then again, she decided as she caught Rusty and Cade's expressions, maybe daytime would be a problem too.

Ah, well. Perhaps they'd take lessons from Pretty Boy and find themselves a blind canyon. There was the Cattleman's Ball coming up in Salt Lake City. Rusty didn't usually go, but she'd made reservations this year. Letty didn't know whether it was because of Pretty Boy or Cade McCall. She wasn't sure that Rusty did either. The Cattleman's Hotel wasn't a blind canyon, but maybe it was close enough.

Letty uncapped the bottle of Tundra Tonic Eugene had shared with her when he came back to the house earlier. She poured a dollop into the stew and began to hum.

On Monday morning Eugene drove Pixie into Coyote Wells to school. Cade left shortly afterward on an undisclosed mission, and Rusty rode out, then came back about midmorning and floundered around the house like a fish out of water.

"What's wrong with you, Rusty?" Letty finally asked. "How come you're not out there working with the men?"

"They're rounding up the south herd to be dewormed, and I decided that I'd check back and see if Cade would like to join us. He says he wants to learn about the ranch. Besides, I'm not going to treat him like—" She hushed. *Like my father did me*, she was about to say. "I mean if you have confidence in a person, they ought to know it."

"You're absolutely right. But he isn't here. So you might as well get on about whatever it is you need to do."

"Oh, you're right, Letty. But I thought that Cade would be here, and we'd . . ."

"Well he ain't. And you ain't—at least you ought not—not until that judge gets them papers ready. When is he coming over?"

"Tonight, after supper."

"And what is this contract going to say?"

"Well, it deals with the six months we're going to take to . . . get acquainted. Then if I'm—you know—pregnant, we'll set up alternative plans for . . . . then."

"I see," Letty said cautiously, "and what is Cade supposed to do in the meantime, other than get acquainted with you?"

"Well, he can ride. He can be with his daughter. He can—where is he anyway? It isn't safe for him to go out on his own."

"I don't know. He didn't say. Asked if he could use the Jeep and left. Somehow, from what I've seen of Mr. McCall, he'll find something to do. I think he can take care of himself."

Rusty hated to admit that the same thought had occurred to her. Occupying his time hadn't been a prime consideration when she was making her plans. She'd thought he'd act like one of the hands. But it had become obvious right away that that wouldn't be a good idea. The men naturally looked to him for instructions. Rusty had to hand it to him. Cade had seen what was happening and backed off.

Lunchtime came and went. The meeting with Judge Meekins was confirmed, but still no Cade. Rusty met with Doak and discussed the breeding schedule for the new bull. The timing of his arrival was perfect. Most of the cows had calved in late December and January. They would soon be ready to breed again. But Rusty didn't want to take any more chances with Pretty Boy on the open range.

With the use of a teaser cow, they could fool the bull and they'd be able to inseminate the herd artificially without using nature at all. Nine months from breeding, she'd find out how successful Pretty Boy had been. And with any luck at all, the new cows would be able to range farther with less water than this generation.

When Pixie arrived home from school, she came flying into the kitchen, books in hand, relating with excitement the events of her first day.

"Letty, there are lots of other boys and girls in my class. We have recess and movies and a lunchroom," she explained. "Oh, Daddy and Eugene and I are going to like living here." She turned to Rusty, question marks in her eyes, "Mrs. Rusty?"

"Oh, you don't have to call me that," Rusty said warmly. "You can call me—" but she didn't know what to say. Mother? No, she wasn't Pixie's mother. She wasn't Pixie's daddy's wife. "Rusty," she finished quietly.

"Okay, Rusty. Is my daddy back? Eugene said he had to see the doctor."

"'Doctor'?" Rusty frowned. Was Cade feeling sick and hadn't told her? Now she was really worried. Leaving Pixie and Letty in the kitchen, Rusty walked into the study and sat down behind the desk. Being at loose ends was new to her. In fact, she couldn't remember ever wandering aimlessly around the house in the middle of the afternoon. If she'd been back in Salt Lake City, she'd have found that bar again. In fact, there was no reason why she couldn't make herself a drink. She always kept liquor in the house.

She removed a glass from the cabinet and began studying the labels on the bottles beneath. What did one put in a mixed drink? She hated to admit that she didn't have any idea. Neither her father nor Ben thought a woman should drink. So she never had. A glass of wine with a meal was acceptable, an occasional cocktail at a party, but drinking at home for no particular reason was unknown to her.

Finally Rusty took one of the bottles and poured an inch into the bottom. To that she added seltzer water and stirred it with a swizzle stick. She didn't have ice, and she didn't want to ask Letty to fill her ice bucket. She'd take it straight. That's what the hands did when they went into the Coyote Saloon.

Taking a big gulp, Rusty swallowed, and swallowed, and swallowed. She was on fire. When the liquid hit her stomach, it set off a tidal wave of sensation that cut off her breath and made her gasp.

Behind her she heard a low chuckle.

Cade was standing in the doorway, trying unsuccessfully to hold back his laughter. "Do you mind if I join you?" he asked casually, and strolled over to the liquor cabinet.

Rusty managed to still the volcano erupting inside her stomach and nodded. "Of course not."

"What are you drinking?" He picked up the bottle and read the label. His eyes widened.

"Rum? Well, I prefer a snowbound night with my rum, but if that's your choice, okay."

"Truth is, I don't know one bottle from the next, McCall. I'm not much of a drinker."

"You called me Cade earlier. I like that better. It sounds more intimate."

"And you called me Rusty. I like that better too. Why don't you . . . mix us a proper drink. I don't think this one is very good."

"Why don't we ask Letty to make us some hot chocolate instead. I think I'd rather see a future mother drinking something nutritious. Liquor won't be good for the baby."

"You're so sure there's going to be a baby?" Her voice was breathless, and she made no effort to stop it.

"I'm sure," he said, replacing the bottle and removing the glass from her hand. "Aren't you?"

She thought she said yes. But as his lips claimed hers, she wasn't sure. In fact as she melted into his arms, she wasn't sure of anything except that she'd been waiting for this all day.

In the dining room Cade saw that his plate had been moved from the end of the table to the middle of one side.

"This is a lot better," he said, once again walking around her chair to assist her. "I like your dress."

"I didn't move your chair," she muttered, promising herself to speak to Letty about her meddling. And she liked what Cade was wearing too. His jeans had been starched and pressed. The black soft sweater he'd pulled over his head had mussed his damp hair slightly and clung to his upper body shamefully. Here and there she caught the flicker of light in a droplet of water he'd missed when he'd dried himself after his shower.

Rusty looked down at the soft pink dress she'd worn and wished she'd made another choice. Pixie had chosen it during a quick visit they'd shared just before Letty called her to supper in the kitchen. The simple high-necked jersey dress hugged her breasts and nipped her waist like a display gown on a dress form, emphasizing every curve of her body.

"Moving you was Letty's idea." Rusty sat down in her chair and scraped the legs as she slid it forward in a desperate attempt to avoid the touch of Cade's hands. She was too late.

Cade stood for a moment, his hands on her shoulders, then leaned down and planted a light kiss on the side of her neck. "Ah, Letty—a woman after my own heart."

"Fine," Rusty snapped, fighting the sensation of his lips touching her skin. "Give it to her. She's a fool for valentines and romance." It seemed that every time she gave in to his kisses, she began to have doubts about the ease with which he claimed them.

"Sorry, darling," he whispered from behind her

as he straightened up. "It comes as a package deal."

After that, conversation was strained, then non-existent. Finally Letty, in exasperation, slammed down their plates of baked chicken and dressing, and put her hands on her hips in a threatening manner.

"Now listen here, you two, it's obvious that Cade isn't into basketball and Rusty doesn't know one end of a football field from the other. You can't exchange recipes or tips on cows. I don't know what it is about you and mealtime that addles your brains, but if you don't get whatever it is out of your systems and enjoy the food I prepare, I'm going to turn that wild man Eugene loose in the kitchen and let *him* cook for you."

"'Wild man'?" Cade repeated, a twinkle in his eye. "He said that you two would get along."

"Beans and biscuits?" Rusty said at the same time in horror.

Rusty and Cade looked at each other and began to laugh.

"You're right, Letty," Rusty agreed. "There's no point in letting our differences spoil your food."

"'Differences'? I don't think we actually have any differences, Rusty," he said. "I think that our problems are very much the same problem. Perhaps we could skip dessert for now and go into the study. I'd like to hear what that judge is going to put into the agreement."

"Good idea, Cade." Rusty stood up and skirted the table. "When Judge Meekins arrives, Letty, please show him into the study. If you'll go on ahead, Cade, I'll join you in a moment. I promised Pixie that Glenda would tuck her in."

"'Glenda'?"

"Didn't you know? I'm Glenda, the good witch. And if you'll excuse me, I'm going to follow the yellow brick road to Oz."

"Is that why you're wearing the pink dress?"

"Yes," Rusty admitted with a blush. "Pixie said that Glenda always wears pink."

Cade didn't comment. He paused in the doorway, basking in a rare feeling of contentment as he watched Rusty walk down the hall. Gone was the long stride and swagger that he'd seen that first day. Instead, the woman climbing the stairs gave off an aura of gentleness and well-being that made the whole house feel content.

Cade held back the urge to follow her. It was important that Rusty and his daughter find a common bond if this relationship was to become permanent. He'd thought that Pixie might rebel at the idea of another woman intruding into their lives. But he was continually amazed at his daughter's ability to accept what came and adjust to it. It had taken him a long time to learn to do that. And just when he'd thought he had the system licked, Rusty came along to knock it cockeyed.

Glenda, the good witch. Leave it to Pixie to put a name on a thing and turn it into a treasure. Cade stood in front of the fireplace with both hands braced against the mantle. Good witch or bad witch, Rusty had certainly cast a spell on his heart.

"Cade?"

She'd done it again, crept up behind him, and he'd been so intent on his thoughts that he hadn't heard her. He turned around.

"All done?"

"Yes, and Pixie sent you this." She stood on tiptoes, placed a quick kiss on Cade's lips, and pulled away.

He swallowed hard. "I don't suppose that I could send her a reply?"

"I think you'd better not." They were only inches apart, and Rusty knew that she ought to step back. The judge was due any minute, and now was not the time to let herself get carried away. "I think what we need is some of Eugene's Tundra Tonic."

Rusty tried not to think about Cade's kiss. But she couldn't step away. Her legs felt liquefied. Her breasts burned to touch Cade's chest, and she felt a great aching need as she speculated on how Cade's hard body might feel against her, nude and aroused. She took a step forward. If she didn't hold on to something, she would fly out into the night.

"Cade?"

What might have happened next was erased by a knock on the door.

"It must be the judge," Rusty said tightly, and stepped away.

"Probably," Cade agreed, forcing himself to walk over to the window and think about snowstorms. He touched the windowpane and felt its cold touch against his skin. Control, he chastised himself. It wasn't working. Ice storms. He'd focused on sleet and avalanches. So focused was his concentration that the man who entered the room was subjected to Cade's back for a long unexplained moment.

"Sorry I'm late, Rusty," he was saying when Cade turned around. "Had a flat tire on the way." He gave Rusty a quick kiss on the cheek and walked into the room. "Is this the temporary husband?"

"Yes." Rusty took one look at the expression on

Cade's face and stepped between them as Cade moved around the chair into the light. "Judge Meekins, I'd like you to meet Cade McCall."

The judge was short, red-faced, and abrupt. He glared at Cade with suspicion. "Well, you aren't what I expected."

"That seems to be the general consensus."

The judge gave a startled shake of his head and moved to the desk. "All right, let's have a look at the agreement, though I don't know why you feel the need to have one. In my day, if a woman wanted a baby, she got married and then got pregnant. I don't think much of reversing the order."

He placed his briefcase on the desk and snapped it open, pulling out a sheaf of legal-size papers. "I'll just hit the high spots here. You can look them over and sign them now, or I'll pick them up tomorrow."

"Go ahead, Judge, tell me what they say." Cade walked around the high-backed chair pulled up to one corner of the desk. He needed something in his hands, something he could focus on.

After the judge rattled off the terms of the agreement Cade forced himself to hold on to the chair, before saying forcefully "There are two very big problems left unanswered. First, I won't be a kept man—for anybody, for any reason. If I stay here, I have to have something useful to do."

Rusty looked puzzled. "I have no problem with that, Cade. What do you have in mind?"

"Obviously I don't know anything about cattle, but I can learn. But I do know about water supplies and pipelines. I believe that I can contribute, and I want the right to work included in the contract. Is that agreed?"

"Agreed. What's the second thing?"

"That may be more difficult." He walked around the chair and came to stand beside Rusty. With little regard for the judge's surprise, Cade turned her to face him. "I was abandoned by my father. I won't do that to my child. Any children I have will have a mother and a father, or they will never be born."

"But—but—but," the judge stuttered, "that means a permanent marriage, and that wasn't part of Rusty's plan."

"Not necessarily. It only means that I intend to be a father to my children. The details can be worked out if the need arises. Will you agree, Mrs. Wilder?"

"Yes," she finally whispered. "If there are children, we'll work out those details to your satisfaction."

"Eh—well, I suppose that I can rewrite the temporary marriage clause, if you're sure."

"We're sure," Letty said, striding into the room, dragging a broadly smiling Eugene behind her. "And we're the witnesses. You need witnesses, don't you, Judge?"

"Eh, well—well, yes." The confused man's face turned even redder. After a moment he turned to the papers and began to make adjustments. "Now, if the parties affected would just initial the changes here—" he waited for Rusty and Cade to focus their attention on the legal document and sign, "and here—and here."

"Where do I make my X?" Eugene said seriously,

as he wrote Eugene Philip Wesley Manderville, III, in the space indicated.

"The third?" Letty chortled in disbelief. "There couldn't have been a first, and a second. You have to be an original."

"Ah, madam, there are many sides to Eugene of which you are not yet aware. But never fear, you will be."

"That's what I'm afraid of," Letty said. "Let me show you to the door, Judge. Do we keep those papers, or do you need to file them somewhere?"

"Each of the agreeing parties keeps one, and I have one for my files."

Letty ushered the judge from the study. Eugene assisted by carrying his briefcase.

The study was suddenly empty and quiet.

Rusty took a shaky breath and wondered what she had done.

Cade turned back toward the fire to cover his own confusing thoughts. He'd forced her into agreeing that the marriage would be real, if there were children. And he didn't know if he could ever fit into Rusty Wilder's world. He didn't know that he wanted to. What he wanted was the woman. What in hell had he done?

"Cade? Why did you go to see the doctor? Are you sick?"

"Doctor?" He let out a deep breath. "Not the doctor, Rusty, the veterinarian," he answered absently. "I went into Coyote Wells to look over a map of the area and stopped by the vet on the way back."

"Why? I have all the maps you need in the office."

"Not the maps dealing with water tables and drilling rights."

"That's a waste of time," Rusty said. "Every rancher in the valley has spent a fortune drilling. Why'd you stop by Will Fleming's?"

"I thought it would be good to get acquainted if I'm going to live here. We talked about bulls and tranquilizer guns. I'm a pretty fair shot, and if there's a way to control your bull with tranquilizers, I thought I might be able to help out. I also found out—"

If Rusty had stopped to think, she would have realized that what he said made sense. But she couldn't. All she heard was that he had taken it upon himself to go to town and meddle in the business of running Silverwild without talking it over with her, before she had a chance to explain Cade's presence.

"I suppose you told Will that you were here as—to—to be my private stud? That must have given him a big laugh. You couldn't have picked a more perfect person to share our plans with. You see, Will Fleming was your biggest rival. If I'd belonged to his church, we probably would have married long ago. As it is, he almost had your job. Maybe I should have chosen him."

She hadn't meant to say that. She didn't even think of Cade in those crude terms. As soon as the words left her mouth, she knew she'd made a mistake. Cade McCall would never be anybody's stud. He was a man, a proud man, who'd given up his plans for his own life to make a better home for his child. He was exactly the kind of man she'd choose as a father for her child. And what was she giving him? A cruel, mean-minded shrew.

"Cade—" she began.

"Forget it, Mrs. Wilder," Cade said coldly. "You

didn't choose him. You picked me, and I have a contract that I intend to hold you to. Either way, I figure I can't lose. I'll be married to the wealthiest woman in the state, and I'll have an unlimited supply of sex." He picked up his contract and folded it carefully. "I'd better take good care of this. It's worth a lot of money."

He strode out of the room without a backward glance.

Rusty watched in stunned disbelief. A log in the fireplace broke and set off a shower of sparks.

What had she done?

Six

The night was silent. Not a quiver of movement broke the quiet; not a shiver of wind brushed against the window. To Rusty it was as if the valley had pulled the mountain on top of itself to hide. She paced the floor restlessly.

Not since Ben's death had she felt so lost and out of control. Her careful plans had vanished in a blaze of fire. From the moment she'd met Cade McCall in the airport, she'd been caught on an emotional roller coaster—feeling wild anticipation one minute and desperate anxiety the next. She'd allowed Cade McCall to overshadow every plan she'd made and every thought she had. Instead of Silverwild being the focus of her existence, Cade McCall had become her first thought in the morning and her last thought at night.

Never before had she met an obstacle she couldn't see a way around. She'd prided herself on being able to define the problem, look for an answer, and implement the steps necessary for a solution. But now Cade was the problem, and the steps she needed to take to get past her fascination with him entailed the very action she'd hired him for—sharing his bed. And now he'd taken that option away from her.

Across the open courtyard opposite Rusty's room, Cade strode back and forth, racked with a raging consternation he couldn't shake. For the first time since he'd come home and found Janie gone from their apartment, he was floundering. Even learning about Pixie and assuming responsibility for a child he didn't know he had was nothing compared to the cloud of indecision that had fallen over him now. He didn't know why he'd insisted on the marriage remaining intact. He'd thought once that he had been in love. He'd been wrong.

Loving homes with peace and satisfaction were myths. This time he wasn't even married to the woman, and he was churning with anger, with frustration. He felt great concern for his child, who already viewed Rusty as Glenda, the good witch, who gave pleasant good-night dreams. Could he control his wild desire for a hot-tempered witch who was determined to rule her own little kingdom?

If only he could find an answer, a temporary answer, one that would give him time to work out another solution. Not only for himself and Pixie, but for Eugene as well.

A temporary solution. A vision of Rusty flooded into his mind. There was a roaring in Cade's ears that blocked out all rational thought. He tried to draw in a deep calming breath, but his heartbeat seemed to accelerate. With a roar of fury he pushed open the door that lead to the patio and plunged into the icy night air. He peeled off his sweater and dropped it to the floor, welcoming the feel of the icy air on his chest. Ice and cold he could deal with.

He leaned his head over the bannister and drew in a long desperate breath, then lifted his head, his eyes catching the light in the room across from him.

A shadow was moving back and forth—pausing, turning, then pacing again. He could feel Rusty's distress as if he were standing in the room with her. They were tearing each other apart. She too was in great pain, and he was the cause. Before he gave rational thought to his actions, he broke into a run around the patio, hugging the U-shaped house. He reached her door and turned the knob.

It opened.

Rusty stopped, wide-eyed and surprised, her lips mouthing his name. "Cade."

His hands were suddenly on her shoulders, stroking the heat of her skin. He moved his finger-tips around her neck, found the zipper beneath her hair, and pulled it down, letting the dress puddle in a pink cloud at her feet. Lacy white underwear was torn away, and she was standing before him, dewy white skin, fiery red hair tousled wildly, green eyes glazed with passion he'd never expected to see.

His hand, still resting on the nape of her neck, lifted the heavy mane of her hair, threading it through his fingers, across her shoulders, and down her breasts. His rough fingertips circled one nipple, studying her as if he'd never seen a woman's body before.

"Beautiful," he whispered, "every part of you. A flame ready to flare up at my touch." His other hand caressed her body, lifting the breast, holding her so that he could lean forward and rub his chest against her. He felt her shudder and hoped that it signaled the heat that constantly simmered beneath her deceptively cool exterior.

"You," she whispered, threading her hands in the rich fullness of his hair. "I want to touch you." Her hands plunged down his chest, lingering at the waist of his jeans before unsnapping them and sliding her hand inside, touching him, circling the solid evidence of his desire. He groaned, then pulled her hand away.

"Cade, please." She caught his waistband in her hands and pulled his jeans down, freeing him to thrust forward in blatant arousal. She gasped, then reached for his briefs and pulled them down legs that were corded with muscles.

Cade's body, still cold from the patio, was like ice against her feverish need. His feet were already bare. He stepped out of the jeans and gave them a kick, sending his and her clothes across the floor in a wild tangle of lace and denim. As their bodies touched, every sensation was more acute, more alive, more demanding than she'd ever known, and Cade was responding in kind.

Fire met ice.

The sizzle was almost audible. Cade muttered a garbled curse and claimed her lips with a violence that was met with equal force. Probing, possessive, arching tongues demanded and received as Cade dropped to the floor, bringing Rusty to the carpet beneath him. For a long moment he raised himself on his elbows and glared at her, not in gentle need but in a fury that was fed by passion.

Then he lifted himself over her and stared down into her eyes. A blaze of a thousand sensations ran through his veins and settled with a thud in his heart. Even as he devoured her with his eyes, he knew that whatever happened in their crazy bargain, he was in love with this woman. He wanted her, yes. But he wanted her for always, and six months of making love wouldn't be enough.

Beneath him, Rusty felt as if she were being devoured by the wild passion of Cade McCall. There wasn't a part of them that wasn't fused. There was no plunging in and withdrawing. Even as he pulled back, she lifted herself and moved with him. His hands, now beneath her body, held her to him so they were never apart. It was the rhythm of life, of giving, of total surrender.

And when the climax came, it ripped through them like the reverberating shudder of an avalanche in the wilderness, rolling on and on, then gradually dying in the wonder of its splendor.

Their making love was more than a simple touching, it was a merging of two souls.

And then he pulled away.

The powerful sensation subsided, the heat cooled and left two people, still touching, yet more separate than before.

Rusty opened her eyes into the dark depths of Cade's—acceptance? Defeat? She couldn't be sure. She only knew that they'd overpowered each other, extracting and claiming what might have been refused if they hadn't been on fire.

"You've won," he said as he pulled away and stood up. "I can't stay away from you. You've hired yourself a man. But if this relationship has a chance of working, sleeping with you won't be enough. I have to find a place for myself here."

"Cade, I want—"

"You want. I want. You've branded me with fire, and we'll destroy each other if we don't find a common ground. I'll give you your six months. For now, I'm just like that bull—bought."

He pulled on his jeans and slipped out the door into the night. Rusty felt moisture in her eyes. She should have felt triumph at her success, but at this moment she felt only sadness. She crawled to her bed and lifted herself into its protective covers, snuggling deep inside like a small child afraid of the dark.

She felt drained. She felt ashamed.

Then if flickered, a tiny warm sensation somewhere deep inside. Even as she acknowledged its presence, she felt it begin to glow. Cade was wrong about her having taken his soul. She'd only borrowed it for a while, to comfort hers and give it life. She pulled the other pillow into her arms and buried her face against it.

Cade. She wanted him again, here, in her arms. And she'd find a way to make it so. Rusty Wilder McCall—the name had a nice ring to it. Maybe a compromise would be possible. Will Fleming would never have fit, in her imagination, or her arms. In the end he'd married his childhood sweetheart, Ann-Marie. They belonged together.

Maybe she and Cade McCall belonged together

too. Maybe not. But Cade McCall was real. She smiled. Cade McCall was a lot like Pretty Boy—awesome.

Cade didn't leave the next morning. But he might as well have. For the next week he spent all his time on the range with Doak and the men, leaving before Rusty got up and returning late at night. He found every crook and corner of the distant range to ride in during the day. He ate with the hands, and where he slept she wasn't sure.

Rusty let him go. She knew that she had to let him find a way to live on the ranch. Finally she was obligated to send word to Cade by Letty that the dance they were attending was to be a formal affair. She offered to order a tux, but Letty said that Cade's reply was that he understood and he'd make his own arrangements. He did, however, ask for use of the truck when he needed it, and Rusty agreed.

Until the plane was repaired, Rusty was forced to rely on the Jeep or remain on the ranch. There was a large black limo that had been used when Ben was alive, but Rusty hadn't ridden in it since the funeral. She spent her time in her office, working on the computer, entering figures, making business calls, and trying to decide how best to convince her fellow ranchers to make use of Pretty Boy's skills. Hefty stud fees would go a long way toward easing the shortage of ready cash in her bank account.

Breeding a new line was as important to her competition as it was to her. For it was her water that they wanted for their cattle. It was her water that the melon and wheat farmers wanted too. But she didn't have an answer for that yet.

The spring thaw had already begun up in the mountains. The runoff would soon reach the valley. She glanced out the window. The mountains were like steps with great dry areas in between. The water from above melted, ran across the dry stretch of land too hard for too long to absorb it, and found its way to the river. If somehow that water could be captured without interfering with the flow of the river, many of the problems between Rusty and the other ranchers could be solved.

As Rusty peered out the window, she caught sight of Pixie dancing across the courtyard toward the corral. In her hand was an after-school treat, a cup of milk and a piece of jelly cake. She reached the fence separating the corral from the rest of the barnyard and stopped. Rusty could tell she was talking to someone, but the corner of the house kept her from seeing who was beyond the fence, until—

"Pretty Boy!" The bull ambled into view, gave a snort and pawed the ground for a moment, then stuck his head between the posts and began nibbling at the cake in Pixie's hand. Rusty ran out the patio door and began to cross the yard in a rush.

She decided not to call out. Any word might set the bull off, and Pixie could be hurt. Even now, as hard as they'd tried, nobody had been able to get a hand on the wildly excitable animal. Yet now he seemed perfectly content to lick Pixie's hand and listen to her chatter. Rusty drew to a stop.

"And then, Pretty Boy, my daddy and Miss Rusty are going to get married and have lots of babies. We'll live here forever, and I'll never have any more bad dreams. Rusty is a good witch, you know. She makes the bad dreams go away. If you would be nice, she'd make you smile too. Now drink your milk." She giggled. "I sneaked some of Eugene's tonic in it. It's good for what ails you."

The child held out the cup, and the bull began slurping noisily. "That's enough now. I have to save some for the kitties." Pixie patted the animal on the head and began walking down the fence toward the barn. "I have to go now, Pretty Boy. When the kitties are strong enough, I'll bring them out to play with you."

Rusty watched as Pixie disappeared into the barn. The bull stood watching, too, then gave a satisfied swish of his tail and walked slowly away. Rusty wouldn't have believed what she'd just seen if she hadn't been there. The bull was gentle and easy with the child. But then everyone responded to Pixie that way, including herself.

Turning back to the kitchen, Rusty found Letty stirring something on the stove and singing loudly. It took Rusty a minute to identify the song as "I'm Getting Married in the Morning."

"Letty, I hate to interrupt your concert, but do we have a litter of kittens in the barn?"

"If they're still alive. Doak said they came night before last, puny-looking little things. Their mother crawled in there half starved. He tried to feed them, but he doesn't think they look too good. Why?"

"Pixie appears to be feeding them."

"Oh, yes. She asked for extra jelly cake and milk. Those little things can't eat yet, but I didn't think it would hurt her to try."

"I'm afraid it wasn't only the kittens she was feeding the cake to."

"Oh? Well, if she wanted seconds, she only had to ask."

"No, it wasn't for her either. She fed that cake to the bull. And you know what? He licked it from her hand."

Letty dropped her spoon and turned to Rusty in alarm. "You mean that creature from hell you brought here?"

"That's what I said. Do you by any chance have any of Eugene's Tundra Tonic in here?"

"Eh—well, maybe I do. Why?"

"I want to have a look at it."

Letty looked a bit guilty as she reached under the sink and pulled out a long-necked brown beer bottle with a cork. "Humm, seems a bit lighter."

Rusty took the bottle and opened it. She took a big sniff. There was little odor. She pursed her lips, took a deep breath, and turned the bottle up, taking a sip of the clear liquid. There was little taste until the liquid hit her stomach, and then she knew.

"Moonshine! Eugene's Tundra Tonic is pure moonshine. I didn't know anybody made this stuff anymore."

"I'm sure you're wrong," Letty protested. "It's a special tonic Eugene brews from Alaskan herbs and berries. He got the recipe from the Eskimos."

"I'll just bet he did. No wonder that bull became so docile. No wonder he ate out of Pixie's hand. He's becoming addicted." Rusty slammed the bottle on the table and strobe out the kitchen door toward the barn. She'd just have a little talk with

Eugene, and with Doak, and with Cade. This was no way to tame a wild animal.

By the time she reached the barn, the warm glow in her stomach had intensified, setting off waves of fullness that undulated throughout her system, forcing her to slow her step. Inside the barn she heard Pixie's voice and followed it to a back corner of the hayloft.

There she found the child with the mama cat in her lap and the kittens nursing contentedly. The mama cat was lapping the last of the milk from the cup that Pixie was holding.

Rusty kneeled down beside her. "Pixie, do you know what's in Eugene's tonic?"

"Yes, ma'am. It's the essence of life. He puts it in a bottle, and when a person, or an animal is feeling poorly, he gives them a dose. They always feel better. Look at the mama kitty. She's purring because she's very happy now."

Rusty took a long look at the cat. She did appear to be happy. She certainly didn't look like the puny cat that Doak had described. Neither did her kittens, whose coats shone with a slick glow. Of course, that was a possible result of drinking moonshine. After all, it was made from sugar and fermented materials, all ingredients that could build up an animal's strength. Rusty shook her head. She'd have to go to Cade. There was no other answer. She couldn't have Eugene parceling out alcohol as medicine.

She stood up, ruffling Pixie's hair as she moved away. For now, that would have wait. She had to get ready for the Cattleman's Ball. She'd take up the issue of the Tundra Tonic afterward—

providing Cade remembered that he was to be her escort.

Three hours later, as Rusty walked down the hallway to the center steps at the curve of the U-shaped house, she met Cade McCall at the top.

He'd remembered.

Cade McCall in jeans and boots was spectacular. But Cade McCall in a tuxedo was mesmerizing. Except for his white shirt everything was black— his jacket, his trousers, his formal boots. The only color he wore was his tie, a flame-colored satin scarf looped into a knot at the neck and falling down to touch the top of the V of his brocade vest. He looked like a man of danger. She could only stare at him and wait.

Cade walked slowly toward Rusty. Tonight she was wearing a royal-blue lace and sequin dress that covered her as though it were her skin. Only because of the slit in the side that reached almost to her hip could she walk. Like a woman from a painting, she wore her copper-colored hair piled on her head, held there with ebony Spanish combs. She wore no jewelry. It would have paled into obscurity in contrast with her hair and the vibrant color of her skin.

Even as they stood—opposite, silent, observing— he could sense something different about her. She was proud as always, defiant, but there was an uncertainty that touched him. He released a deep breath. There was no stopping the wrench inside his chest. Every time he came close to her, it seemed to rip a little more. The pain had long ago given way to a kind of wonder, afraid yet to make itself known but simmering there until Cade was ready to acknowledge its presence.

"You're very beautiful," he said.

"You're very handsome," she answered.

"You won't be ashamed to be seen with an oil-field roustabout?"

"Not if you're not ashamed to be seen with a clumsy ranch hand," she said softly.

He held out his hand. "I'll be the most envied man there."

She placed her rough hand in his rougher one. "If you let one of those man-hungry women lasso you, I'll—I'll—"

"What will you do?"

"Maybe I'd better put my brand on you right now," she said, and pulled both his arms around her as she lifted herself on tiptoes.

"Oh, how do you plan to do that?"

"Like this." When she kissed him, he knew that she was right. He was being branded. It might not be visible, but the brand was there, and it glowed brighter with her every touch.

"Daddy! Daddy! You look like Prince Charming," Pixie called out from the bottom of the stairs.

"Eh, yep." Eugene beamed broadly. "Reckon he does look pretty good. 'Course he's got a good-looking woman to look good for. You two had better come along. Your pumpkin is waiting."

"Aw, Eugene." Pixie grinned. "That's not a pumpkin out there. It's a big shiny car. And Doak's wearing a uniform too."

Reluctantly, Cade pulled away, sliding his hand properly under Rusty's arm. "Shall we go, my dear?"

"Of course, Prince. I can't wait to see what kind of pumpkin Doak's driving."

"Don't say a thing. Eugene and Doak have been

working all day. And it wasn't easy because the wash water kept freezing until they decided to bring kerosene heaters inside the garage to warm the place up. They may have to repaint the walls, but this car shines."

Rusty slid her arms into the fur coat that Letty was holding while Cade donned the dark overcoat that Eugene held out. The addition of a black Stetson made Cade just about the most exciting man that Rusty had ever encountered. For the first time in her life she couldn't wait to attend a social event in the city—and show Cade off.

They stepped out into the crisp night. Snow was beginning to fall, sprinkling the night with huge soft flakes that fell like glitter in the headlights of the car. It was the Cadillac, as bright as new. Doak, standing beside it, was wearing a black suit and a captain's hat. As a chauffeur, he presented an interesting picture. But as a conspirator, he was beaming in pleasure.

Doak assisted them inside. Climbing in the front, he made a production of closing the dividing glass and plunging the back into darkness by closing his door.

"Privacy," Cade commented wryly, and glanced out the window. "Is the snow likely to interfere with our drive?"

"No, we're only driving over to Coyote Wells. We'll catch a ride in with Will Fleming in his plane. Flying will be easier than driving."

Until now, Cade had felt good about the evening. Since he'd learned that Will Fleming had been his rival, he wasn't so certain how he felt. From a country boy back in Tennessee so many years ago, he'd come a long way. His trip into Salt Lake City to rent the tux had been interesting. The young woman in the store knew at once what he wanted and helped him put together the complete outfit. She even ran down to the mall to a department store to find the silk scarf they used as a tie. He bought the boots and Stetson with the last of his personal funds. Escorting Rusty to the ball might work. It would make it plain to everyone that Rusty Wilder was the future Mrs. Cade McCall, along with the other little surprise he'd arranged.

"Tell me who I'm going to meet."

"Well, of course there's Will Fleming. But you've already met him and Ann-Marie, his wife."

"His wife? You considered an affair with a married man?"

"I didn't say I considered. I just said he offered. And he wasn't married at the time."

"And what else am I likely to have to deal with?"

"You mean at the ball?"

"That too. But what I'm primarily interested in is how you expect to explain me."

"I won't. You're with me. That's all they need to know."

"I don't think so. The way you look tonight, I don't want to have to fight off any jealous liquored-up old boyfriends."

"'Old boyfriends'? That's a laugh. When I was in the seventh grade, I was already a foot taller than any boy in class, and by the time they grew up, I wasn't interested anymore. Somehow, going from bean pole to beautiful was never meant to be."

"I find that hard to believe, Willadean."

"God, don't call me that. That's all I need."

Cade glanced at Doak in the front seat. He

couldn't see, and the partition kept their conversation private. Cade slid his arm across the back of the car seat and touched Rusty's shoulder. "I sort of like that name. It makes you seem human."

"You think I'm not?" She turned to look at him, imagining in the darkness that she could see the dark eyes and serious drawn brows that came with the crooked smile she was sure he was wearing.

"You know what I thought the first time I saw you, standing in the middle of that airport?"

"Yes—I mean, I don't know."

"I said, 'Thank you, God, for not sending me a Mack truck.'"

She let out a laugh and leaned back into the curve of his arm. "Is that what you were expecting?"

"Either that or some love-starved widow with six chins and a beard. What I got was fire and brimstone, a woman that any hot-blooded man would kill for."

"And are you hot-blooded?"

"I am now. Before I came here, I was accused of being an ice man, distant and hard." He put his other arm around her waist and pulled her across his lap at the same time his lips found the bare skin of her neck and began to move wickedly across the top of her breasts.

She gasped. "I can say part of that is true, anyhow." She wriggled against him, feeling him pressing against her, and whispered, "There is definitely nothing—soft about you."

His hand slipped up beneath her coat to the top of her dress and beneath it. "I'm damned glad that isn't true about you. I like your soft parts." He was speaking in a gruff voice, barely above a whisper.

He found her nipple, stiff against his fingertips, trembling beneath his touch.

"Hummmph." Doak cleared his throat. "The Flying Gull is just ahead."

Cade let out a long reluctant breath. "Do we have to go, Redhead?"

"We do." Her voice wasn't any stronger.

"All right," Cade agreed. He drew Rusty's dress back over her breasts and she forced herself to sit up. "But there's one thing I think we ought to make clear, right up front."

"What's that?" Rusty took a tube of lipstick from her evening bag and tried to repair the damage she'd done to her makeup. She thought a moment, pulled a tissue from the bag, and turned to wipe the evidence from Cade's mouth.

"You're mine."

"I'm what?"

She stopped, caught by complete surprise at his words. After what had happened a few nights ago, she'd expected him to disappear. He hadn't. But he hadn't been back to her bed either. Now he was suggesting that they make their arrangement public. She was confused.

"You're the future Mrs. Cade McCall. I want people around here to know that, and I think you ought to have an engagement ring to make it official." He pulled a ring box from his pocket and handed it to her.

"But Cade, you didn't have to do this. I mean, what if I don't get pregnant? What happens in six months?"

"We have six months to find out, don't we? And in the meantime, I've decided that I'm going to earn my pay. I've never taken on a job that I didn't do well. I don't intend to start now."

"But you didn't have to do this. I mean with a ring. What do I care what all these people think about me? I've always done what I wanted to do, and they don't expect any different." But she did. His gesture touched her. He understood more than she wanted to admit.

"I think you do care, darling. I'm going to help you make them sit up and take notice of the future Mrs. Cade McCall, owner of Silverwild Ranch."

Darling? Rusty liked the sound of that word. She leaned forward and flicked on the overhead light. Inside the box she found an engagement ring. A gold filigree setting held a stone that was unlike anything she'd ever seen. It was a ruby, yet its color was almost fire red, and it caught the light and shimmered like a meteor disintegrating as it fell from the sky.

"Oh, Cade, it's beautiful. It's the most beautiful thing I've ever seen. How could you—I mean it must have been very expensive."

"It was, and you'd better not lose it. It isn't paid for yet."

"Oh, where did you buy it? I'll send a check." Rusty immediately wished she could take back the words. Cade's expression changed from intensely tender to thunderous.

"No! I don't know exactly how you intend to pay my salary, but I assume I get one. I'll take care of the ring myself. Now hold out your hand."

Rusty complied contritely, watching as Cade lifted the ring from the box and slid it on her finger. It felt hot. It would be, for it had been in his pocket. He'd warmed it up for her, concealing it next to his body. She caught her breath and lifted her eyes to meet his.

"Thank you, Cade. This is the loveliest thing I've ever owned, and I'll be the most envied woman at the ball."

"Oh, it's not that big."

"It isn't the ring," she confessed shyly as she placed her hand on his rough cheek. "It's because I have you and everybody there will want what I've got. But you're mine, Cade McCall," she said in her normal to-hell-with-the-world voice. "I've already put my claim on you."

Cade waited a long time before he answered her. Then the only answer he could give was the truth. "And you've already put your mark on me too. Eugene says that I've been branded with fire."

Will Fleming was tall and blond. He directed the transfer of luggage (that Cade hadn't known they were carrying) and his passengers into his plane, larger than Rusty's. There was another passenger already inside, a blond-haired, blue-eyed beauty who introduced herself as Will's wife, Ann-Marie. She took one look at Cade, and her eyes opened wide.

Will and Ann-Marie were already dressed in dinner finery. After Will gave his final instructions to his men on the ground, he strapped himself into the pilot's seat and began the checklist to leave. Less than twenty minutes later they were landing at the Salt Lake City airport and transferring to the black limo waiting at the runway.

Once inside the limo, Rusty moved close to Cade. He was pleased that she did so naturally, as if they truly belonged together, as if they were a couple.

"That's the Mormon Temple," Ann-Marie said, calling Cade's attention to a stark white block-long building bathed in light.

"It's spectacular," Cade admitted. "Like a castle in a fairy tale."

"It's the heart of all Mormon life," Will said seriously. "Parts of it are never opened to outsiders. Ann-Marie and I were married there."

Cade took Rusty's hand and absently rubbed his thumb across the engagement ring as Ann-Marie pointed out the Sea Gull Monument; the Beehive House, home of Brigham Young, the Mormon leader; and the Eagle Gate, which used to be the entrance to Brigham's estate.

"You know the story about how the sea gull came to be the state bird?" Will asked.

"No, I don't believe I do," Cade admitted, wishing they were already at the dance so that he'd have an excuse to hold Rusty in his arms. Gone was the uncertainty and tension that had plagued them for the last few days. Tonight he was just taking his lady out on the town. He squeezed her hand, giving every indication that he was attentive to his host. Only Rusty knew that he was absently rubbing his middle finger back and forth across her palm. "Sea gulls in the middle of Utah?" Cade's voice was disbelieving.

"Yep," Will answered. "They thought the Great Salt Lake was the ocean. A plague of crickets swept across the valley. They were destroying the first crops that were to carry Brigham Young's people through the winter. Suddenly a flock of sea gulls appeared and ate the crickets. The crops were saved, and the gull became our state bird."

"Enough sight-seeing," Ann-Marie interrupted. "Rusty, Will told me that Cade is from Alaska. I suppose that he—oh my, look at your ring, a ruby—" She stopped herself and looked up at Rusty with excitement in her eyes. "Rusty, that's an engagement ring, isn't it? You and your mystery man from the land of ice and snow are engaged."

"Yes, ma'am," Cade said, lifting Rusty's fingertips and planting a kiss across her knuckles. "We most certainly are."

"Will, did you know that Rusty was getting married?"

"Yes. Well, not exactly." Will leaned back and gave Cade a measured look. "But Cade did drop by the other day. We had a little talk about raising cattle and breeding bulls. Have you set the date?"

"In about six months," Rusty answered.

"And then again, maybe sooner. It all depends on—well, let's call it fate," Cade answered with a long measured look at Rusty.

"Yep," Ann-Marie said smartly, "he's a goner, all right. Well, I can understand you importing him. Will was the last eligible bachelor in Utah. And I got him, didn't I? How'd you find Cade?"

Rusty blushed. "Let's say if you're looking for a man, you have to look in the right place and use the right kind of inducements."

Ann-Marie tilted her head and examined Rusty carefully before turning to Cade. "Oh? And what kind of inducements did you have to offer?"

"We met in an airport," Cade answered, "and she

didn't need any bait. Let's just say I'm partial to bossy redheads."

The limo came to a stop under the famous porte cochere outside the imposing red brick structure with the unlikely name Little America Hotel and Towers. The doorman, unexpectedly resplendent in a black tuxedo, hurried to open the door.

Cade left the car first, taking Rusty by the hand. As she raised her head and stood up, he pulled her close and whispered wickedly in her ear, "I'm very partial to bossy redheads with long legs and beautiful big—"

"Bank accounts, McCall," she said under her breath, teasing him back and a dream that she's willing to share.

Seven

"This is some place," Cade commented as he took in the stained-glass dome overhead.

"The Towers is nothing like the Cattleman's Hotel, where they used to have the ball," Rusty said in disgust. "My daddy would have hated this."

"Your daddy didn't like change, Rusty," Ann-Marie said. "If it were up to him, we wouldn't even have a ski resort in Utah. He and Ben Middleton both wanted you and everything else in the state to stay the same—no tourists, no farmers."

"You're right," Rusty agreed. "He thought the range belonged to the cattle."

Cade kept silent as the foursome moved past the huge fireplace and through the lobby. Walt Wilder hadn't liked change. He wanted to keep Rusty the same too. To that end he'd made her feel plain, ordinary, even picking a safe husband for her. But anybody seeing Rusty tonight would know that was no longer true.

Cade smiled. A sexy new dress wasn't the only change Rusty had made. Old Walt would probably turn over in his grave if he knew that Rusty had found herself a husband.

Cade watched the startled looks of the other guests as they caught sight of Rusty Wilder. He could already discern that they hadn't expected Rusty to attend, that the woman they were seeing was a Rusty they'd never seen before. One man after another did a double take, only to be reprimanded by the woman on his arm as he stood, gaping. Rusty smiled blithely at everyone. Only Cade knew that she was holding his arm in a death grip.

"Easy, Redhead," he whispered. "I'm here to protect you from the wolves. Anybody who gets too close has to deal with me."

"Is it that obvious?" Her voice was huskier than usual. Gone was her in-charge air, leaving a smile that was tentative.

The woman on his arm might look like the richest woman in Utah, but he could recognize that out-of-your-element feeling. He'd known it often enough as a mountain child in Tennessee. "Not to anybody else. But from where I stand, I'd say that you'd rather take on Pretty Boy than this group. Why are we here?"

"Because I need to hire Pretty Boy out for stud and I have to convince some people here that it's a smart moneymaking move. Nothing breeds success like looking successful. That's what my daddy always said."

They reached the coatroom, where a sulky blond claimed Cade's overcoat and Rusty's fur. The look she gave him promised more than a claim check if he was interested. Ann-Marie immediately stepped inside and found someone to talk with, leaving Will on one side of Rusty and Cade on the other. Together they stepped into the doorway and surveyed the noisy ballroom.

A hush fell over the crowd. It lasted only a moment, like a temporary glitch in a sound track, then the crowd exploded into new bursts of conversation.

A beefy red-faced man broke away from the crowd and started toward them. "Rusty, good to see you girl. Where've you been keeping yourself?"

"Russ?" Rusty straightened her shoulders and preceded Cade into the room, separating herself from him with a shudder. "I've been meaning to give you a call."

"Oh? You've decided to accept my offer to buy that little piece of rock in the north corner?"

"No. What I had in mind was making you an offer."

The jovial man looked at Rusty shrewdly, cutting his eyes from Rusty to Cade and back again. "Oh? You're not going to sell it to Dale Briggs are you?"

"No, my offer has nothing to do with that. I don't intend to sell any of Silverwild. What I want to talk to you about is my new bull."

"Yeah, I heard about the ugly devil. Ought to be a good match for them buffalo up at Howard's place. Howard, come over here. Rusty's got a deal for you."

Will Fleming, who'd followed them, snagged a canape from a passing waiter and eyed it with a grimace. "A Cattleman's Ball ought to serve steak," he commented.

A tall, thin older man detached himself from the

group he'd been talking to and walked over to meet Rusty.

"Howard Chandler," he said holding out his hand to Cade. "Don't believe I've met you, sir."

"Cade McCall, and you haven't."

"A cattle buyer, Rusty?" Howard asked, taking a long look at both Cade and Rusty.

"No. You might say that I've been in oil." Cade took a long look at Rusty. "But I'm looking around at other opportunities." He slid his arm around Rusty's waist and smiled at her possessively.

Rusty allowed herself to lean into him. She hadn't expected that meeting these men would be so intimidating. She'd had business dealings with them over the years, but those encounters had been on Silverwild, on her own terms. Now she felt off balance. Except for Cade, whose arm told her that he was there for her. His strength was hers if she needed it. And she did.

There was no question about the man's power. Or his magnetism. Already, Howard Chandler and Russ Long were uncertain. Every woman in the room had been watching him from the moment of their entrance. She'd seen the buzz of attention ripple around the room, and she traced it back to the man holding her. She could certainly understand their reaction.

She'd been worried that bringing Cade here was expecting too much. After all, if she couldn't convince the other ranchers to use Pretty Boy, what could his presence add? He wasn't even a rancher. Silverwild was her responsibility, and so was its future. Truthfully, Cade McCall wasn't here to deal with the cattlemen. He was with her, not because of what he represented but because she needed him. All her life she'd tried to please her father, with little acknowledgment of her efforts. After Ben's death she'd decided that she would please no one except herself. And tonight—tonight it pleased her to be Cade McCall's woman.

Cade stumbled slightly. He decided that if Rusty could have found a way to climb into his pocket, she might well have done so. He couldn't tell whether it was from uncertainty about the men she was talking to or the women she kept eyeing uneasily in the crowd beyond. In either case he figured that his duties as a fiancée suited his purposes as well as hers. He dropped his gaze and gave Rusty a deep private smile as he slid his warm hand possessively up to her shoulder, pulling her back so that he could look into her eyes.

Shyly she reached up and caught his hand, squeezing it as openly as she returned his hungry look.

Russ looked at Howard and back to Rusty. "Oil, huh? Well, if you didn't lost your shirt, maybe we could talk sometime, McCall. Rusty has all the land and water, but her French cows can't compare with my herd."

"Not at the moment, perhaps," Cade answered evenly. He felt, rather than heard, Rusty's inaudible intake of breath. "But the new bull is going to change all that. You'd do well to have a look at him, before his stud fee gets too high. In the meantime I'm hungry, darling. What about you?"

Rusty allowed herself to be led away. "Why'd you do that?" she asked. "We could have talked more about Pretty Boy."

"Always make a man think you don't want what

he's offering. It makes him more interested in what he's turning down."

At the buffet table they were joined by Will and Ann-Marie. Filling their plates with little chunks of steak, potatoes, and melons, they found a seat and ate. Rusty and Ann-Marie identified various VIPs, including some people they'd gone to school with.

Rusty only picked at her food. Will complained that they ought to be eating real steak and potatoes, not little finger foods. Ann-Marie reminded both men that they'd elected to skip dinner and arrive in time for the ball.

"Speaking of the ball," Cade said, "I think I'll dance with my lady."

Rusty found herself being turned expertly toward the dance floor, Cade's hand guiding her through the crowd of people until he found a spot near the center of the floor.

"You don't have to do this. I'm not much of a dancer, Cade," Rusty whispered anxiously between lips planted in a tight smile.

"Doesn't matter. I wanted an excuse to put my arms around you. Just lean against me and sway."

"I'm not sure this is a good idea."

It wasn't a good idea, Cade decided as Rusty complied. At thirty-seven it had been a long time since his body had responded so instantly to a woman's touch. But then a woman like Rusty had never been his before. Suddenly his body was fourteen and had ideas of its own.

"Cade?" Rusty broke off and gaped as she felt him harden against her.

"Sorry, darling," he said blandly. "I can't seem to control myself when I touch you. You're the boss. Give me an order. What shall I do?"

"I don't know. What do men normally do?"

"Depends on the woman, darling."

"Why are you calling me that?" she whispered. "There's nobody listening now."

"Because I want to. Does it bother you?"

"Yes! You make me crazy. I can't think."

"There comes a time, Redhead, when feeling beats hell out of thinking."

He was right. Rusty stepped forward, draping both arms around his neck. "Not here, McCall. Let's go. Allowing your feelings to show may come easy to you. But I've never . . . I mean, I don't think I can stand being stared at one more second!" She began moving backward with great determination.

This wasn't embarrassment, Cade decided. Suddenly Rusty was really upset. He didn't know why. He'd been caught up in the aura of holding a beautiful woman in his arms, a woman with great green eyes that promised more than even she knew, and he'd let himself go too far.

Cade swept her around until they reached the glass doors behind her. He turned the knob, and in a second they were outside the ballroom on a terrace. Rusty tore herself from his arms and moved over to the rail. Beyond the hotel the lights of Salt Lake City glowed in the darkness. A sharp wind curled around the building and swept across the terrace.

"Are you all right?" Cade asked.

"Yes. I mean, I think so."

"I don't understand, Rusty. What happens when we touch is a constant surprise to me. I don't normally react to a woman every time I hold her. But together we seem to explode."

"I know. I'm sorry. You must think I'm crazy. It's just that nobody but . . . I mean, I've never had a man like you be so—so obvious—before. I feel like a fool."

Cade pulled off his jacket and placed it across Rusty's shoulders. "You're cold." When she didn't protest, he slid his arms around her and pulled her back against his chest, clasping his hands around her waist.

"It's all right, darling," he said softly. "It's normal, when two people are on the same wavelength."

"Maybe," Rusty conceded, allowing herself to relax a bit. "But it doesn't always work that way."

"Rusty, have you been to the Cattleman's Ball before?"

She tensed, trying to find the words to answer. "Once, the first year that Ben and I were married."

"What happened?"

"Ben and I danced once. Then he just disappeared and I had to go home alone."

There was more here than Rusty was telling. Cade couldn't imagine any acceptable explanation for Ben's deserting his young wife. "Your husband disappeared? What does that mean?"

"I didn't understand then. Later, I did. We hadn't been married long. You see, to Ben, I was like a daughter. He could never see me as a wife. It wasn't that he didn't want to. He tried, but he never"—her voice dropped to a whisper—"could make love to me. That night, we were dancing. He—well, the same thing happened to him. Later he started to drink. There was a woman at the dance. He went home with her."

"The bastard!" Cade tightened his hands around her stomach.

"No, Cade. He was just drunk." She turned inside his arms to face him. "I'm sorry, Cade. I didn't mean to be so silly in there. It took me a long time to understand about Ben. He never meant to hurt me. He simply couldn't live with loving me."

"I do understand," Cade said in a low voice. "I'm having something of the same problem myself. About those people inside. If you brought me here to make some kind of statement, I can understand that."

"I know it was foolish, but I was always Walt Wilder's girl. I never fit in with the women. I didn't know how. Since Ben's death, they've tolerated me, but they've openly laughed at my ideas about running my ranch. I decided tonight that I'd come here and show them all that I was as much a woman as any of them, and as good a rancher too."

"Rusty," he said tenderly, "don't you know that you're the most beautiful woman in the room?"

"No. My father always said I was gawky, like my mother. She was never able to fit into Salt Lake society. She died when I was a child, so I never learned either."

"Hell, who wants a lady? I'll take a hellion any time. Don't you know that what you're seeing in there is pure jealousy from the women and pure lust from the men? You're the best-looking, sexiest woman in the state, Rusty Wilder, and you're mine."

Her look was pure astonishment. "But my father said—"

"Your father was a fool, and as for your husband, I think I feel sorry for him. He must have fought a real war with himself about you. I think that in some crazy kind of way, he won."

"Cade, I don't believe a word you're saying, and I understand even less. How can the fact that Ben went off with another woman and left me to be the laughingstock of the ball mean that he won anything?"

"Because if he'd stayed, he'd be thinking the same thoughts I am, and marriage license or not, that would have been morally wrong to him."

"Ben was a fine man, Cade. Only he drank too much. He never meant to hurt me."

"But I think he did. I think your father made you feel awkward and Ben made you feel unwanted, and they both did it to protect you."

"I don't understand."

"Your father knew how beautiful you were going to be. You'd be a target for every fortune hunter in the state. He wanted to make you tough enough to stand on your own two feet, but he wasn't sure that he'd succeeded. So he married you to Ben. And Ben had a real problem. He must have wanted you something awful. But he couldn't let himself love you as anything more than Walt's daughter."

"But he was my husband, Cade."

Cade tightened his grip around her waist and took a deep breath. She smelled like sweet flowers in the spring. She felt like sunshine in the winter. Cade fought the overpowering urge rising in his body. He had to stop himself from reacting to her touch. He couldn't go around the rest of his life holding his hat in front of his lower body.

"I know," he murmured. Cade turned Rusty around, pulling her into his arms. For a long time he just held her. "I know how he felt. The man must have been made of iron. How could he hold you and not do this?"

Even the air felt charged as Cade lowered his head. His hands gathered her to him. He angled her head back and kissed her, murmuring explicit words of desire that he didn't even know he was saying. But she didn't pull back. She molded herself to him, demonstrating her own needs by the hungry way she returned his kisses.

"Oh, Cade. Cade." She called his name softly, and the calling became a plea that was more urgent with every thrust of her tongue inside his mouth.

Then the door opened, and a loud swell of music blared out into the night.

"Rusty, darling," Ann-Marie Fleming said as she closed the door, shutting off the music. "I hate to be the one to break this up, but some of the men are having a cigar in the bar. I've been sent to ask Cade to join them."

Cade pulled back, stationing Rusty between himself and the woman as he tried to still his racing pulse. Another minute and he'd have been making love to Rusty right there on the freezing patio. He took a deep breath.

"Thanks, Ann-Marie. But a cigar with a bunch of ranchers can't even begin to compare with the company I'm keeping. Give them my regrets, will you?"

"No!" Rusty said hurriedly. "Tell them that Mr. McCall won't be joining them, but I'll be in shortly. I'd like to talk to them."

"Rusty darling, this may be 1991, but the last woman who joined the men for cigars was from the Coyote Wells Saloon, and she came out of there with a new car and a diamond as big as your ruby engagement ring. I don't think they'd think too kindly of your interfering."

"Damn!" Rusty pulled away and took a step toward Ann-Marie, who shook her head and went back inside. "This is where it all takes place, Cade. All the under-the-table deals between the bankers, the cattle buyers, and the government officials who dole out the water rights. I won't let them close me out. I have to get in there."

Cade caught her by the shoulder and stopped her. "Rusty, I don't think you're going to do anything but make your cause worse if you intrude. I'll go."

Rusty stopped and glared at him. "What do you mean, you'll go? You don't know anything about cattle, or water, or bank loans. What can you do?"

"I'm not sure. But at least you'll be represented. I'll be a little mouse with big ears."

The earnest look on his face kept Rusty from refusing. She frowned sternly. "All right. Just be sure that ears are the only thing big you carry in there. The women inside might never let you get to the bar."

"They will, Redhead. Remember, I told you that I had to earn my keep. Now, this is where I'm going to start."

"Cade—" She didn't know what to say. How could she say what she wanted to accomplish without telling him the entire truth? Nobody knew how desperate she was to make Silverwild the ranch it could be. Nobody knew how dangerously low her cash reserves had dropped. She needed a loan or the promise of stud fees to keep the ranch going in style. Cade would have to help her with the men in the bar without knowing the truth.

"Okay, Cade. I'll stay out here for a while. Then I'll go powder my nose and wait for you."

"I don't want you out in the cold, darling. I want a woman who's warm and willing, not an icicle in a shroud." He gave her a light quick kiss, and together they went back inside. Rusty handed him his jacket and let her eyes play down his body and back.

"What do you want me to do in there, Redhead?" he asked seriously.

"I don't know. Just play it by ear, I guess. I—I trust you, Cade."

"No suggestions for handling the situation?"

"None," she said softly. "Just don't get lost. I won't go home alone."

"You won't have to, Willadean," he said solemnly. "Not ever again."

The bar was a private room set up by the hotel for the cattlemen. There were no women present. Even the bartenders were male.

Cade accepted a drink and declined a cigar. He nodded to the men being introduced: Howard Chandler, Russ Long, and Will Fleming, whom he already knew. Yep, they were gathering, the vultures. He just wondered how they intended to pounce and why.

"McCall," Howard Chandler called out, "come and meet the real money in our group—T.L. Landers and Thomas Paxton."

"Gentlemen, Cade McCall. He's engaged to Rusty Wilder."

Cade blinked. He hadn't expected the word to get out so quickly. He shook hands with the two men. "More ranchers?"

"Hell no," Russ Long snapped, then pasted a false smile on his face. "They're bankers. T.L. is the president of First Oklahoma Bank and Trust, and Thomas runs Gull Savings and Loan and the largest melon farm in the state. If you need somewhere to put your oil money, these fellows will be glad to take it off your hands."

"Oh, I think my money is well invested right where it is," Cade said dryly. A rented tuxedo and a down payment on an engagement ring was a fine investment from his point of view.

"Yes," Howard Chandler observed, "that's what old Walt thought, too, when he married Rusty's mother. She had the money. He had the land. Trouble was, he didn't give her room to breathe. Always thought she gave up and died just to get out from under his thumb. Never thought Rusty would stick it out after Ben died. Guess there's more to her than old Walt thought."

"So you're engaged to Rusty Wilder," Thomas Paxton commented with a hard look at Cade as he turned to the bar. "I'm not surprised."

"Oh? Why?" Cade would liked to have questioned Howard more, but the confidential tone of Paxton's voice seemed more important. Cade turned and followed the banker, planting his foot on the rail and turning his back to the other men who'd turned to greet a late arrival.

"Well, considering the state of affairs out at Silverwild I can understand why she'd find herself a rich husband."

"What makes you think that it isn't me who's finding himself a rich wife?"

"Because," Thomas said quietly, "I know how desperate her situation is. Whatever your arrangement with Rusty is, McCall, you'd be wise to advise her to take advantage of my final offer."

"Oh? What's that?"

"I'll give her the loan, all right, but only if she gives me the water rights to the runoff at the top of the valley."

"I thought a banker kept his business confidential."

"This isn't a banker talking now, McCall. This is Thomas Paxton, farmer. And I'll do whatever it takes to get that water."

"And what would you do with it?"

"I'd figure out how to trap the runoff from the spring thaw in that blind canyon of hers. Then I'd have enough water to irrigate. Water, Cade, cheap water—that's the real money in the state."

"I was in that canyon last week. There isn't any water in there."

"Not yet, but there will be."

"I'll take your word for it, but I don't know that I can convince Rusty to do anything. Besides, if saving that water is such a good idea, why hasn't she done it herself?"

"The best way to do it is to build a dam. But that takes cash and expertise. Besides, she's as foolish about that land as old Walt was. He didn't want to stop the runoff from reaching the river and the ranchers downstream, and neither does she. Trouble is, too much is lost that way."

"I can't say that I've seen much need for it on Silverwild," Cade commented.

"Not yet. But wait until midsummer when the grass all dies and there isn't enough to feed her herd. Then the cows start dying of dehydration and she has to truck water to them from a river twenty miles away."

Cade didn't know how to answer the man. But he was beginning to understand Rusty's buying that bull. A more drought-resistant strain of cattle could be crucial. But if there was water to be had by building a dam, that was important, too, and that was something he knew about.

"I'll think about it, Paxton," he promised, and turned back to Howard Chandler and his group. Howard glanced at Paxton and back at Cade. The expression on his face was one of concern. Cade caught the imperceptible shake of Paxton's head. So the offer was a joint undertaking.

When Howard offered Cade a second drink, he declined. He'd found out what Rusty wanted to know. And he'd found out what he needed to know too. "No thanks," he told Howard, "and my lady has been alone far too long. I wouldn't want her to think I've been kidnapped."

"Well, she ought to be experienced at that," a voice came from the back of the room. "Old Ben walked off and left her the last time she came. At least he was a man who knew how to keep a woman in her place."

Dead silence.

Cade turned, his teeth clenched as he searched for the source of the voice. Before his gaze the men stepped back, forming a wedge that focused on one man standing at the end of the bar. He was probably drunk, from the looks of his loosened tie and unbuttoned vest.

"My name's McCall," Cade said as he walked slowly toward the man. "What's your name?"

"It's Tobe Freeman. What's it to you?"

"I like to make certain that a man knows who I am before I hit him. Seems friendlier that way."

Cade drew back, and before anybody quite knew what had happened, he'd planted his fist against the side of the drunk's face with a resounding thud. With a little nod of approval, he watched the man slump to the floor.

"Thanks for the drink and the conversation, gentlemen." He turned and started back toward the door, stopping as he opened it. "By the way, all of you know about the bull Rusty bought. Well, he's going to breed a new strain of drought-resistant cattle. But, just to cover our—bases, as a wedding present, I'm going to build my wife a dam. So if any of you want to talk confidentially about your water needs while you're out checking Rusty's new bull, I'll be around."

The dance floor was still crowded. Only the older men, the selected inner circle of money and prestige, were invited to have cigars in the bar. The younger men were still dancing.

Will came alongside him. "I'm glad to see Rusty and Ann-Marie getting along so well. Ann-Marie was worried. She's pregnant," Will confided, "and I think she'd like a friend close-by to talk women things with."

"Congratulations. Rusty and I plan to have a family too. She told me that the two of you were friends . . . once."

"Don't worry about me, Cade. I never was any

competition for you. Rusty wasn't in love with me. It was all on my side. There was a time when I would have married her in a heartbeat."

"She said there was a problem with your religion. What were you, Fleming, some kind of priest?"

He laughed. "No, I'm a Mormon, and we aren't allowed to marry outside our faith. I was willing to forget that, but Rusty knew it would be a mistake. She was right. Ann-Marie and I are perfect for each other."

Cade smiled. He thought a close friendship with a woman was new to Rusty. Ann-Marie would be good for her. Rusty, too, would need a friend when they had a child.

"Cade." Rusty looked up anxiously as he reached her side and put his hand on her shoulder. "How'd things go in the bar?"

"It was very interesting, but not nearly so interesting as an after-dinner drink with you."

"Yes," Ann-Marie agreed, "but I think I'd rather have a banana split with mounds of whipped cream. What do you say we find an ice-cream parlor and splurge?"

"We could," Will said agreeably, "but I think that Rusty and Cade would rather be alone. Why don't we all get out of here? Let's see what Room Service has to offer in this hotel?"

"Room service?" Cade questioned.

"Sure, we're all staying overnight. Didn't Rusty tell you? Ann-Marie booked two rooms. One for us and one for you two. Maybe this was to be a surprise," Will confided privately. "I think Rusty may be a little shy about you. Old Walt kept a pretty tight rein on her when she was a kid."

Shy? Cade thought that might be the right word. Ben had ducked out on her. Maybe Rusty had been afraid that he wouldn't be here either. Wild horses couldn't have driven him away. Tonight Rusty wanted a romantic evening, not a completed job assignment. Cade grinned. A room? Overnight?

Grinning foolishly, Cade put his hands in his pocket and rocked back and forth on the balls of his feet. If it hadn't been so obvious, he might have whistled. Damn, he liked Salt Lake City and its people. He felt good, very good. Better than he had for a long time.

Rusty watched as Will swept Ann-Marie around and walked away with his arm tight around her waist.

"Well, I never!" Rusty said in disbelief.

"Neither have I, darling, but we're going to. Come on, Champ. We're going to see a clerk about a key. By the way, how do you feel about banana splits?"

"I can't say that I'm real fond of them," she admitted as Cade approached the reservations clerk.

"Give yourself some time," Cade whispered. "I think you're going to acquire a taste for them."

Ten minutes later Cade was tipping the bellman and locking the door to their room behind him. He turned back to Rusty with a wide smile. "When did you intend to tell me about staying over, darling?"

"When I . . . after I was sure that everything was going all right. And don't call me darling."

"Why not? I think that everything is going to be very much all right." Cade began to remove his clothes, one piece at a time, one step at a time, until he had backed Rusty across the sitting room, into the bedroom, and against the king-size bed.

"What are you doing?"

"I'm about to get to work, boss-lady. I've got a big job to do and only six months to do it in." He turned her around, found the satin tie that held the see-through chiffon across the top of her dress in place. He untied it, kissing a trail around her neck and down the V between her breasts as he unzipped the gown and peeled it from her body.

As his mouth reached her bare breasts, he lifted his eyes and grinned. "No bra? No wonder you had to have that little piece of net on top."

"Oh! You! I know my breasts aren't as big as Ann-Marie's."

His dark eyes stared at her breasts—small, pink, and hard-tipped. "Your breasts are perfect." His fingers went to one nipple, touching it, watching it tighten into a small rose-colored ball. He caught it, lifting, caressing boldly. "I like the black stockings," he whispered as he peeled them down her incredibly long legs. "I like this too." He caught his finger in the skimpy triangle of black lace and played back and forth beneath the band.

"Oh, Cade." She groaned. "I wanted so very much to please you."

"You please me very much." His lips parted, and his breath came quick and hard. "And I want to please you. Do you like my touching you?"

"Yes, oh, yes," she said huskily. "Do you like me to touch you?" Her hands went to his chest. This time he didn't feel cold. She ran her fingers through his dark chest hair, leaning forward to brush his chest with her breasts.

Cade caught his breath as she leaned back and

for a moment thrust her pelvis against him—
against the hard part of him, now throbbing
against her. He ripped the lace panties from her
body and ran his fingers through the rust-colored
hair beneath.

Cade caught Rusty's upper arms, looking down
into green passion-filled eyes. She might not know
about seduction, but their great need for each
other was leading her into paths she'd never trod
before. The last of his reason deserted him as his
hand slid to her bottom and lifted her, bringing
those fiery curls against his stomach and up his
abdomen as he claimed her exquisite breast in
this mouth.

"When we have a child, will you nurse him?"
Cade asked as he pulled his mouth from one
breast and sought the other.

"Yes, I want that—very much." Her voice was
suddenly soft, shaking. "A child," he'd said. "When
we have a child." Would their child be hungry for
her as Cade now was? Would he take her nipple
roughly, demanding? She moaned, clasping her
legs around his waist as she thrust herself reck-
lessly against him.

Only vaguely did she realize that they were on
the bed, Cade on his back, his hands were moving
over her, pulling her against him so that he was
pressing intimately against the valley into which
her whole being eagerly awaited his penetration.
She was going out of her mind with wanting him.

"Oh, Cade, it feels so good, so right! I never knew
it could be like this between a man and a woman."

"But we're not just any man and any woman."

Cade's mouth was touching. His hands were
probing, exciting her body. He could feel her aban-

don as he loved her, forcing her need higher and higher into a blazing torrent of passion that teetered on the explosive edge of release. He stood, bringing her with him as he ripped the bedclothes away.

"No," she whimpered, stopping him momentarily, "don't, don't stop, please!" She lifted herself against him, finding his mouth as she arched against him.

This time he laid her down and fell across her. This time he didn't hold back, plunging deep inside her. This time he felt her heart beat deep inside the cavern of her desire, and the soft warmth of her locked onto him and throbbed in expectation.

She began to move.

"No, Rusty, don't. I can't hold back. Be still."

She stopped. But the tense grasp of her muscles couldn't stop the spasms vibrating inside.

"Oh, Cade. Such pleasure. I never knew that a woman could feel such pleasure."

"Rusty, you're so sweet. You're so warm and beautiful." He closed his mouth over hers and felt the ripple of heat begin. Though she tried not to move, like a storm at sea the waves rolled in, far away and distant at first, then growing stronger and wilder, sliding against each other, it came— intense pleasure that grew and grew.

"Cade," she cried out, and there was no more stillness.

Feverishly, Cade thrust himself into her over and over until he felt the aching spasms of release sweep over her. And then his own crashing climax overtook him, and he could only hold on and feel and feel and feel . . .

Cade went still. He was still inside her, but suddenly he was heavier, wet with perspiration and breathing deeply. Her arms were still around him, and she began to rub his back as if he were a baby who needed comforting.

"Spectacular," she whispered. "Simply awesome, McCall." She touched his neck, his arms, his hair, loving the feel of him. She knew that what they'd just shared was more than mating. He didn't have to tell her they'd climbed the mountaintop and they'd done it together. Now that they'd reached the other side, she found she was still clinging to the wonderful feeling.

Moisture collected in her eyes. She wanted to laugh. Instead she was crying. She felt him move. Her body reacted with a protest. It liked what it had captured. She knew now she wanted Cade McCall to stay forever where he was, in her arms, inside her body, inside her soul.

"I'm too heavy," he whispered, lifting his head to look into her eyes.

"No, don't move. I like you inside me."

He touched her face with his fingertip. "So beautiful," he whispered, "loving you, being inside you."

Her face glowed in the lamplight. There was a flush across her cheeks, a wonder in her eyes. He came up on his elbows and leaned down to kiss her. He wanted to cherish her, to look after her, to give her a whole new world in which he would be the focus.

The spot of warmth deep inside her widened and intensified. It was enchanced by their joining, but it also was separate from it. There was a special softness about it, and the glow from inside washed outward until her whole body felt as if it were shining.

Above, Cade looked down at her with unabashed joy. He could feel her pleasure, over and above his own. And he laughed.

"You don't smile much," she said slyly. "And you laugh even less. I'm glad I make you happy. I—" she held back the rest. She wanted to say I love you. But she didn't. Those words were so final, and she didn't know how Cade would react. Lying here with him now, she didn't want to do anything to change what they shared.

"I wonder—" she started to say, and hushed as her body felt a stirring down below.

"You wonder what?" he prompted, taking her nipple his mouth.

"I wonder if we could do that again?"

And they did—not once but twice more, and then once again just before dawn. As Rusty closed her eyes in sleep, she let herself finish her thought. She wondered if Cade had given her a child. That thought filled her with joy.

A child meant marriage.

And for her, marriage to Cade McCall meant forever.

Eight

The next three weeks brought a steady stream of ranchers to the Silverwild to see Pretty Boy. Each of the men found a reason to stop and chat a moment with Cade.

During the day, Rusty and Doak managed to complete the herd's spring deworming. Pixie stayed underfoot at every turn. With a family and a new school she was thriving. To Rusty, the relationship between the child and her father was a joy to see.

A bedtime story from Rusty soon became part of Pixie's daily routine. As did the nightly disappearance of Letty from the house during mealtime. Eugene apparently was finding his Tundra Tonic an aphrodisiac, for Letty had changed her humming song from "I'm Getting Married in the Morning" to "A Blanket on the Ground."

During the daytime Cade looked at maps, studied books and pamphlets, and made numerous phone calls. He performed whatever task Rusty assigned him in such a way that it seemed to be a joint venture. At night he made glorious love to Rusty, always slipping back to his room before morning.

At the end of three weeks Rusty learned about the place Cade had created for himself on Silverwild. She might not have found out for months, but she had gone into Coyote Wells to check on the repair of the Cessna and visit the doctor. To make her visit to town completely joyful, she decided to stop by the bank on the way home. She could hardly wait to tell Paxton that she no longer needed a loan from his bank. Pretty Boy's stud fees were taking care of her financial problems.

The smile he gave her when she'd finished wasn't a surprise. His reply—"Guess not, with McCall blackmailing everybody into using that bull"—was.

"What do you mean?" Rusty slid to the edge of her chair and leaned on his desk.

He looked at her as if he didn't believe her question. "You don't know, do you."

"Know what, Thomas? You'd better tell me, or I'll move what's left of my account to another bank and tell everybody in town that yours is failing."

"Oh, you don't have to do that, Rusty. I'll tell you. After all, I stand to gain as much as everybody else. It's your water. McCall is going to build a dam and siphon it off."

"Build a dam? How's he going to do that?"

"He's going to make me a partner. He builds the dam and pipeline. I put up the money. We have all the water we need, and we sell the rest. I'll have to hand it to you, Rusty, you've got more sense than I gave you credit for. Even old Walt could never have pulled this off."

She didn't remember leaving the bank. She didn't know when it started to rain either. Cade had found a way to pull Silverwild out of the financial hole, and he'd set his plan in motion without saying a word to her. No wonder he'd been so happy. He'd stayed out of running the ranch, taking her orders and carrying them out like everybody else who worked for her. And all the while he was carefully planning to dam the canyon and sell the water to any rancher in the valley who needed it.

Carrying out her orders like all the other men who worked for her. That phrase kept running through her mind.

What did she expect? She'd started the game, but he was the better player. He was doing the same thing that her father had done to her, giving her an illusion of power by letting her take care of the routine business of ranching while behind the scenes the future of Silverwild was in his control.

She could hardly see the road now. Between her tears and the rain everything was a blur. Lightning cracked the sky. Thunder rolled across the mountains and crashed into the valleys. The rain was falling in torrents. Too bad, Mr. McCall. If you had your dam built, you'd be able to fill it without waiting for the spring runoffs.

And I went and fell in love with the man. I couldn't even advertise and find some man willing to give me a child as a pure business arrangement. She thought about the contract she'd insisted on. More than that she thought about the nights she'd spent in Cade's arms, loving him with every part of her, opening herself up to him. Praying each time they made love that he'd give her a child.

Rusty blinked. She pulled the scarf from her hair and dried the tears from her face. He had intended to stay all along. He was carving out a niche for himself, binding himself to her so tightly that she couldn't shake him loose when she learned the truth. It might have worked if she hadn't already lived that kind of life with her father and Ben.

She should have known. Men were all the same. Like her father he had set out to undermine her position. But Cade couldn't have lied about how he felt. That was real. Even now, knowing what he was doing, she was making excuses for him. For days her emotions had seesawed back and forth, from suspicion to incredible joy and back again.

She wished that Paxton hadn't told her the truth. She'd have to fire Cade, give him his bonus and let him move on. Except that everything had changed. She'd gone and fallen in love with him and with Pixie. She even liked Eugene. And now, according to the doctor she'd just seen, her prayers had been answered. Cade had given her a child. It had apparently happened the first night they'd made love. She was pregnant. There was to be an heir for Silverwild.

She wished—how she wished she'd never heard of Cade McCall. She wished—

Suddenly she was at the entrance to Silverwild. As she drove around the house, she saw horses and riders gathering by the barn. What was going on?

Something was wrong.

Rusty slid from the Jeep and crossed the yard, splashing through the quickly forming mire.

"Doak, what's the trouble?"

But it was Cade who dismounted and directed her into the barn. The expression on his face was more grim than she'd ever seen it.

"It's Pixie. She's gone."

"Pixie? Oh, my God! What happened?"

"Pretty Boy got out of his pen again. Apparently she was worried about him being afraid in the storm. She . . . she went after him."

"Pixie is out there"—Rusty gave a quick twist of her head—"in all this?"

"We're going out to find them. I've sent for Will Fleming. With the storm we don't know if Pixie is with Pretty Boy or how he'll react if we corner him. I want you to stay here."

"No, I'm coming along."

"Not this time, Rusty. I don't want anything to happen to you."

The pain in his voice stopped her for a moment, but the thought of Pixie out there in the storm quickly erased any thought of arguing about his taking over this hunt. He didn't have time to debate, and she wouldn't force the issue. Pixie's life might be at stake.

"Go on, Cade, find her. Bring her back home quickly."

He gave her a hasty kiss and was gone.

Rusty waited until he was out of sight before saddling her horse. Dashing into the house, she passed Letty in the kitchen, making coffee and filling the thermoses she had lined up on the counter.

"Make toast, Letty, with butter and jelly—fast. As much as you can before I get back."

"Sorry, Rusty, I don't have time. Didn't you hear that—" she began.

"I heard, Letty. Make the toast. The coffee can wait." Upstairs she donned warm clothes, ran back down the stairs, and pulled on the slicker hanging by the kitchen door. *Sorry, Cade. You may have all the answers, but this is my land, and I know it better than anybody.*

Letty quickly buttered a stack of toast and spread it with jelly. As she finished, Rusty packed it in a plastic bag.

"I hope you know what you're doing, Willadean Wilder. If anything happens to Pixie because of that creature you brought here, I'll personally shoot him."

"You won't have to worry about that, Letty. Once this is over," Rusty promised as she put the plastic bag inside her slicker and zipped it up, "Pixie and her father are leaving. They don't belong here. I was wrong. A family can't be bought."

She rode hard across the range, following the path that Pretty Boy had followed before. The canyon would act like a funnel, capturing the downpour and the runoff from above. It would direct the stream out through the narrow opening and what was normally a dry dead-end canyon would turn into a raging torrent. Rusty nudged her horse into a run.

But this time Pretty Boy hadn't gotten as far as the canyon. He was standing in the middle of the north range, pawing anxiously at the ground. The men were circled around him.

Rusty rode up beside Doak. "What's happened?"

Doak looked at Rusty with dismay in his eyes. "It's Pixie."

Rusty looked around again. There was no sign of the child. "Where is she?"

"There's an old well there. Walt sealed it off years ago. Apparently the heavy rain loosened the earth. She's down in the hole. We could hear her calling when we first got here. But that bull won't let anybody get close enough to see."

"Oh, no! Where's Cade!"

"Over there."

Rusty felt her heart contract. It would all come down to this. She'd lose the bull, Pixie, and the man she loved all at one time. And it was her fault, all her fault. No matter that she hadn't even known they existed when she'd bought the bull, if she hadn't tried to change things, this wouldn't be happening.

As the rain came down, it seemed to wash her mind clear for the first time. She couldn't send Cade away. She loved him. She'd give him the whole ranch to run as he pleased if that's what it took to keep him. She should have sold the canyon to Thomas. Land wasn't important! People were. Her father was wrong. He'd always been wrong.

It wasn't Silverwild that was important—it was the family. Rusty had been a child when her mother died, but she hadn't been too young to understand that her mother had hated Silverwild. But it was Letty who'd explained the rest. Her father hadn't meant to hurt her mother. But Melanie Wilder believed that she wasn't important to her husband. Her only purpose was to provide an heir. She did—one. There would be no more, the doctor said. When she died four years later, Walt grieved for a while. But six months later he hardly knew she was gone. It had seemed that way, at least to Rusty, for he rarely mentioned her.

It had taken Rusty much longer to get over losing her mother.

An hour ago she had still been blindly repeating her father's mistake, following his plan as if he were alive and directing her life. Cade would provide an heir, and he'd be gone. Except that Cade had refused. He wanted to be a father to any child they created together. The business contract had made that a part of the agreement between the two of them.

She could see the truth clearly now. She should be happy. She was pregnant. But the cost was too high.

Rusty slid off her horse and started toward the man she loved. "Cade, is Pixie all right?"

"I think so. She's scared. I told her not to talk to us. Pretty Boy is already spooked enough. Apparently he thinks he's protecting Pixie. He won't let us get to her."

"Then you'll have to shoot him!" Her response was quick and certain.

"What did you say?" Cade stared at her in disbelief.

"Shoot him. Now. There's no time to stand here talking about it!"

Rusty glanced at the canyon at the end of the valley. By now, the water ought to be pouring into it. In a matter of minutes it would be flooding the pasture where they were standing. She didn't have time to argue with him. Did he really think that a bull was more important to her than Pixie? But there was no time to explain or argue. She had to force him into action.

"When you go into partnership with Paxton and

build your dam, you can buy me another bull. Doak, give me your rifle."

Cade caught her arm. "No. He might fall across the well and collapse it over Pixie. I'm going to try and get him with the tranquilizer gun."

A tranquilizer gun? Not only was he building a dam without her approval, but he was also ready to change the way she operated the ranch. But this time it was Rusty's turn to protest. "No, he could still fall. Those tranquilizers can work pretty fast. What you need to do is get closer. I think I know how to lead him away."

"And how do you plan to do that? Give him an order?"

"I'm going to coax him away with jelly and toast." She unsnapped her slicker and unzipped the parka beneath, producing the plastic bag of mangled toast and jelly. "Just like Pixie."

"No way. He might trust Pixie to feed him toast and jelly, but he doesn't trust you. I don't want you hurt."

"I'm not going to get hurt. Besides, all this is my fault, isn't it?"

Cade took a deep breath. She was right about the toast. It might work. She was wrong about whose fault it was. If Pixie's running after Pretty Boy hurt anybody, it would be his fault. He'd been so busy working out his surprise for Rusty and the children he was going to give her that he hadn't paid enough attention to the child he had.

He'd been able to meet with the representative from the Utah Water Commission and the soil-conservation expert on dam building without Rusty's knowing what he was doing. With a little luck he'd be able to harness any future water pouring into the canyon, and it could be distributed to the other ranchers easily. Not through evaporation and runoffs, but through the same kind of pipeline that he'd spent the last ten years working on.

His plan would solve Rusty's concern over the ranchers' rejection of her bull and prove to her that he belonged on Silverwild, not just for six months but forever.

Like lightning, the truth ran through him. Rusty did care. From the first moment they'd laid eyes on each other, they'd been caught up in a desire that was so intense that it clouded every part of their lives. But he'd understood that a relationship based on sex and nothing else couldn't survive. And he had been afraid that was all they had.

Rusty had just proven him wrong. "Shoot the bull," she'd said. She'd give up Pretty Boy without a thought to save Pixie. Cade began to smile.

The rain was falling steadily, and Cade knew that they had to hurry. He didn't know how deep the well was or how long Pixie would be safe. After her first answer to his call he'd told her to remain silent. Any outcry might spook Pretty Boy and cause a cave-in.

Cade removed his slicker.

"What are you doing?" Rusty demanded.

"Open that bag of toast."

"Why?"

Fumbling inside his jacket, he brought out a long-necked brown bottle.

"I'm adding some of Eugene's Tundra Tonic to the toast. One way or another we need to get that bull's cooperation."

"We also want him to be sober enough to walk. Otherwise he'll be caught in the flood too."

"Oh, we're not going to give him this. The toast is just the carrot we're going to dangle in front of his nose. Besides, Will is bringing a hoist to lift him into the truck."

As Cade poured the liquid into the bag, the rain continued to fall. "I'll try to tempt him into following me away," he explained, including an anxious Eugene and Doak in his plan. "As soon as he moves away from the hole, Doak, you shoot him with the tranquilizer gun. Eugene, you get Pixie."

"What about me?" Rusty said as evenly as she could.

Cade glared at her. "You stay out of the way."

He started toward the bull, waving the bag slowly back and forth, praying that the scent of its contents would overcome Pretty Boy's fear.

It wasn't working. The closer Cade got, the more anxious the bull became. He pawed the earth, lowered his head, and moved it back and forth slowly in a threatening manner.

Rusty knew that Cade was going to be killed. The bull was going to charge. The ground was going to collapse, and Pixie would be buried alive. She had to do something, but what? Then it came to her.

She began to sing "Mary Had a Little Lamb."

The bull slowed his movement and cocked his head.

"Sing, Cade." Rusty called out.

Eugene joined in, followed by Cade's deep voice.

The bull looked around, turning his head one way, then another. He took a cautious step, then another. But his direction took him nearer to the hole. Rusty gasped, heard her voice waver, then picked up the tune again.

Cade rattled the bag. He reached inside and removed a piece of toast.

Pretty Boy took another step, and another, until he was finally past the hole. Doak took aim. Rusty heard the shot from the tranquilizer gun.

The proud bull faltered but kept going. The tranquilizer wasn't going to work. But at least he was far enough away so that Eugene could get to the hole.

Rusty forgot about the bull and went after Pixie. She peered into the hole and saw her on a ledge about four feet down. Below her, the hole was filled with water. Pixie looked up at Rusty and began to cry.

At the sound of Pixie's crying Pretty Boy whirled around.

"Rusty, look out!" Cade's voice and a rifle shot sounded simultaneously. "The bull!"

"No, Pretty Boy!" Rusty screamed, and began to run toward him.

Reacting instinctively to the movement, the bull charged. Bellowing in pain and fear, he lowered his head, catching Rusty between his horns as he collapsed.

"If he'd hit her full force, he'd probably have killed her," the doctor explained to Cade after he completed his examination. "As it is, she just sat down pretty hard. The mud cushioned her fall. She's fine."

Pixie had been reassured that Rusty was fine, and Eugene and Letty were putting her to bed. In the study, Cade clasped a glass of brandy in his hands, swirling the liquid but not drinking. Only now could he release a sigh of relief.

"But she is all right, isn't she?" Cade asked again.

"Oh, yes. As far as I can tell, the baby is fine too. Of course, at this early stage I can't be sure. I'll keep a close check on her for the next few days."

"Baby? Rusty's pregnant?"

"Yes, didn't you know? She said—I'm sorry, McCall. I assumed you knew that she was coming in to confirm it. Less than a month, but she's definitely pregnant. I guess that makes you a lucky man."

The doctor put on his coat and picked up his bag. He held out his hand. "Congratulations."

Cade shook hands. "Thanks. May I see her now?"

"She's pretty exhausted, but I think she'd like that."

Cade wasn't sure. A thousand conflicting emotions clouded his mind as he relived every moment of what had happened. "Kill the bull," she'd said. Then she'd flung herself toward him, screaming "no" as Doak had fired the rifle. In that moment everything changed. He wasn't sure what he'd say to her. They had to talk. They had to make plans. But first he had something to do.

From her room Rusty saw the light flash on in Cade's room across the courtyard. She threw her legs over the edge of the bed and forced herself to stand up. Sooner or later he was bound to confront her. The doctor would have told him about the baby. She knew that, but there was something she had to do first.

She reached for her dressing gown, but her

arms felt too weak to put it on. Her dressing table seemed a mile from the bed as she forced herself to walk to it. From the top drawer she removed an envelope and made her way back to her bed. She'd almost made it when the door opened. Lightheaded, not from the accident but from the coming confrontation, she lunged toward the bed. Somehow her feet got caught in the hem of her nightgown, and she stumbled.

Cade caught her as she fell.

"What in hell are you doing?" He demanded gruffly.

"I—there was something I needed."

"Something more important than the baby?"

This wasn't going to be easy. He was holding her. His arms were tight, and his mouth drawn into a furious line of disapproval. Well, there was nothing new about that. Almost everything she did displeased him, except when they were in bed together. And that would never happen again. She could look into his dark flashing eyes and see that.

"Nothing is more important than my baby, except—"

"Silverwild," he finished for her. "Spoken like a true Wilder."

"I was going to say—you."

"I don't believe you," he said in a low voice.

"I don't suppose I've given you much reason to," she said softly, and let out a deep sigh.

He could smell the scent of her. It filled his nostrils and made him crazy as it always did when they were close. Her softness nestled against him. Just the touch of her, even now, affected him, and he stiffened with burgeoning desire.

God, why was he doing this? She couldn't help

taking chances. It was part of her character. It was automatic. Hell, he'd done the same thing. But Pixie's life was at stake, and he wasn't pregnant.

He wasn't sure of anything anymore. All he could think about was that as close as they'd come to be, she'd never even mentioned the possibility that she was pregnant. Why, knowing that she was, had she risked harm to their child by going out in the storm? Rusty shifted in his arms and lifted her hand to touch his cheek.

"Don't," Cade muttered and jerked away. "Not this time, Willadean."

She flinched, and he wanted to take back the words, kiss away the pain. But he couldn't. All they'd had together was desire. He wouldn't give in to it again. Not now. If he didn't get himself under control in another minute, they'd be in that bed, loving each other again.

No, not loving. Sex, he told himself, pure sex. That's all she felt. She didn't love him. Never once when they'd been together had she ever said one word about love. She'd whispered about feelings, about excitement, about pleasure, but she'd never mentioned love.

Rusty, feeling the tension and hearing his rejection of her, felt her world crumbling. She was going to lose him, and she didn't know how to stop him from going. She'd thought that somehow, when he came to her room, she'd be able to reach him. There was something powerful between them, something overwhelming. It had been there from the beginning; she simply hadn't known. She'd thought that making love was possible without being in love. She'd been wrong. Being in love only made the loving more intense.

She'd fallen in love with him the minute she saw him. Love at first sight? She'd never believed that it was possible. But it had been there from the beginning, and it still was. He'd come into her life and made it secure. Without taking over, he'd been there, steady, backing her up, supporting her. And all she'd done was use him.

He laid her down and stepped back, glaring at her with eyes that seemed hollow and blank. For a long time he merely looked. Then he turned away.

"For what it's worth, Cade," she said quietly, "I don't know any other way to put it except to say that I love you. But I realize that I have no claim on you."

He stopped. In the silence she could hear his breathing.

She went on slowly, determined to say it all, no matter what the cost. "This started with a game, but it's turned into much more. I didn't know how to love, and by trying to keep from being hurt, I've hurt the people I care most about in the world. I'm sorry."

He turned. "So am I, Redhead. You know what's so crazy about all of this? I really love this ranch. I never realized before that a place was important. I've been a drifter all my life, looking for where I belonged. I think I would have been happy to stay. I think we could have had a spectacular life."

Rusty tried to close out the pain in his voice. She understood his pain because it was only a mirror image of her own. She forced herself to go on. "I want you to know that I've ordered Doak to destroy the bull, Cade. He isn't worth the heartache he's caused."

"You did what?"

"I don't care about him. I never did. I only wanted to keep him from hurting Pixie."

"I know that now. But when he butted you, I went crazy. I was afraid for you. Then when I found out about the baby, I was angry, angry that you took such a chance. You could have killed our child," he said slowly.

"Yes. But I didn't. The doctor said that the bull's head hit my chest, just at the moment he fell. The tranquilizer was working. It kept the full force of his fall from touching me. I may not do any riding for a few days, but our baby is fine."

He was having trouble changing direction in his thinking. He couldn't seem to understand. "'Our baby.' That's what you wanted. Now that it's happened, are you still pleased?"

His question surprised her. He was right. A baby had been the object from the beginning. Yet now he seemed to be the person having doubts. There was something about the way he asked that didn't fit with the expression on his face.

"Yes," she answered, and left it there. She didn't know what else to say. That she'd have died before she'd have hurt their child? She would have, but she couldn't expect him to believe her.

"I'd better go," he said woodenly, making no move to leave. "You ought to rest now. If you need anything, switch the light on and off, and I'll come."

He wasn't leaving the ranch, at least not tonight. In spite of all that had happened, he would be there if she needed him. He would keep a watch over her, at least for tonight. She liked that thought, Cade watching over her. Cade caring.

But it wasn't enough. It wouldn't hold him. If by

some miracle he stayed at Silverwild, it would have to be because he wanted her to be his wife, because he loved her. There would be no more games.

Rusty adjusted her nightgown and sat up. She looked at the envelope she was still holding in her hand, then back at Cade. She opened the flap and pulled out the papers.

"Will you come over here, Cade? I want to give you something."

Cautiously, he moved back toward the bed.

"Do you know what this is?" she asked, unfolding the papers so that he could see.

The frown on his face deepened. "The contract. I recognize it. So? Am I to be forced into a shotgun wedding?"

"If I thought it would make you want to stay with me, I might do it," Rusty admitted, "but I don't want to play games anymore. I'm releasing you from the agreement. There will be no wedding, but this is our child and if you wish to have a say in his upbringing and a share in raising him, I won't refuse."

She ripped the papers in half, then again in half, and let the pieces float to the floor. Whatever final arrangement you wish as a settlement will be agreeable to me."

Rusty waited. Her sad eyes seemed focused on a spot just above Cade's boot tops. Gone was the proud self-possessed woman he'd met in the airport. Her face was pale in the soft lamplight. Her proud chin was lowered in defeat as if she expected him to deliver some final blow.

As he stood, watching her, a lovely light seemed to emanate from somewhere behind her, like sunshine in a dark corner. And he knew that was what she'd given him. Sunshine, light—warm happiness that was constant.

Rusty was beautiful. He couldn't understand how she hadn't known how beautiful she was. But she hadn't. It was as if she'd saved that beauty until he'd come along. Then it had burst forth with the force of a new spring.

She'd fought him every step of the way for control of Silverwild and her life. But that inner part of her that no one else had ever touched had been given to him, freely and without restraint. He'd told himself it was because she wanted a child. Yet every time they'd made love, the feeling of togetherness had been more complete, more powerful and it had been harder for Cade to leave.

"Our child," she'd said. For the first time, her child had become "our" child. And then he knew. She meant it. She loved him.

At first Cade smiled. Then he let out a loud, happy yell. Then he lifted Rusty in his arms and whirled her around the room.

Eugene and Letty came running down the corridor and stopped, wide-eyed, in the doorway.

"What's wrong?" Letty asked.

"Wrong?" Cade let out another yell. "Nothing's wrong. We're pregnant, that's what."

"What'd I tell you?" Eugene said, giving Letty an exaggerated nod of his head.

"I never doubted it for a minute," Letty agreed, and closed the bedroom door.

Nine

As the door closed, Rusty was pulling Cade's head down to meet her kiss. For a moment he returned it, then as it began to deepen, he pulled back.

"No, Redhead, you know what this will lead to."

"I hope so," she whispered boldly, running her hand between the buttons on his shirt.

"Not tonight," he said sternly. "You had a bad fall today, and we have to be careful. At least for twenty-four hours. Doctor's orders."

"But, Cade," she protested, twisting her body so that she was touching as much of him as she could, "I want you so much."

"I want you too. But then I always want you." He put her back on the bed and pulled the cover over her body, pausing only to stare at her breasts. His fingers touched her breasts, rimming the dusky aureole, following the path of the veins, now darkening. "You look different. I should have noticed."

Rusty caught her breath as she watched Cade

looking at her body. "That's because of the baby. Sometimes the nipples are painful, the doctor says. Until he's born, I'm supposed to pull on them, rub them to make them tough."

Cade's breath quickened. His touch intensified. "Does this hurt?" He sank down on the bed beside her.

"No. It's very stimulating." She tried not to show him how stimulating his touch was.

"Will being pregnant make you look different in other places?"

"Not yet. I think it's too soon."

Wordlessly, he pulled down the sheet and lifted her nightgown. His fingertips left her breast and moved down to cradle her stomach.

She couldn't hold herself still anymore. A shudder swept over her, and she sat up, pulling the nightgown over her head. She clasped her arms around him, swaying helplessly against him. "Please, Cade. Love me. There must be a way."

He was on fire, but the voice of reason told him that they couldn't. Not tonight. As much as he wanted to be inside her, they couldn't. But maybe there was another way. Yes. He caught the back of her neck, holding her as his lips found hers.

She moaned and arched against him, taking his tongue into her mouth in rhythm with the motion of her body.

Suddenly he stood and stripped off his clothes. Pulling the sheets and blankets away, he knelt down beside her. "Maybe there is a way, Redhead, for me to give you what you want."

She lay back and held out her arms, expecting him to fill her with himself. But he didn't. Instead he moved over her, sliding down so that he was settled on his elbows propped on either side of her chest. For a long time he simply stared into her green eyes, filled with desire.

Then he lowered his head and took her nipple inside his mouth. She was exquisitely hot, swelling inside his mouth. He nuzzled and sucked, as his child would. Letting the nipple go, he moved around the aureole, kissing his way up her neck, across her lips and down to the other breast, all the while touching, caressing her with his tongue.

Tonight he wanted only to give her pleasure. He reveled in the little sounds she made, in the way she moved against him, offered every part of herself hungrily to him. His hand moved down, discovering and teasing her body. His lips followed.

Beneath him, Rusty was on fire. She heard herself whimpering. Her hands dug into his back. Her body had turned into a seething mass of desire. She was in agony. And then his lips slid across her stomach, lower, lower, until he found the center of her desire. She cried out.

"Cade, no. Cade, don't."

"Yes. Let it go, darling. I want to give you what you need."

And then she felt it. That special warm spot deep inside her began to glow. Hotter and hotter, higher and higher. She felt tears stream down her cheeks. Her hands were on the back of Cade's head, pressing him against her, holding him. Her hips were arching, opening herself to him.

And as the red-hot tide burst through her, she felt the very core of her existence open to this man who'd become such a part of her other self.

Then, as awareness filtered over her, she felt his face slide back up her stomach and lie across her breasts. His breathing was rough and uneven, and he was trembling. Her body was slick with sweat, her own heartbeat still erratic.

For a long moment they didn't speak.

"Cade, I . . . I didn't know. I . . . what about you?"

He moved up in the bed beside her, pulling her into his arms. "Don't worry about me. Loving you is enough for me tonight. I just want to hold you to my heart."

He kissed her forehead and lifted her leg across his lower body. Beneath her thigh she felt him, still hard and throbbing. She nudged him with her knee.

"Don't do that, Redhead. There's just so much a man can take before he cracks under pressure."

"Really?" she said with a grin, giving him a deep kiss that increased not only the throbbing but the imperceptible movement of his body against her as well. She began to work her way down his chest, one wicked kiss at a time.

"Don't do this to me," he pleaded, "I'm liable to disintegrate right here in this bed, and little Eugene will never see his father."

"*Eugene?*" She raised her head in horror. "You have to be kidding."

"I'm not kidding. We owe that man a great debt." He gasped as her lips started a downward trail. "After all, he found your ad."

"He didn't force you to stay."

"No, but he knew that I was melting, and he warned me not to let myself drown in the thaw."

But the warning was already too late. As Rusty's mouth found the object of her attention, Cade acknowledged that he'd always wondered what it would feel like to die of pleasure.

And then, in a rush of heat and a passionate groan, he did know.

It was fire and light and explosive passion. It was two people who belonged together. Two people who were joined.

Afterward Rusty raised her head and looked anxiously at the man she loved more than life itself.

"Was it—are you all right?"

He pulled her up over him, laying her face in the hollow of his neck. Now they were together, touching.

"I've never been so all right," he whispered. "Now, go to sleep. I want to hold you through the night. I don't want to leave you—ever again."

"Good," Rusty murmured sleepily, "I have an assignment for you first thing in the morning."

"What is it, darling?"

"I'll show you then," she said, and she slept.

Cade might have slept, but he couldn't be certain. His body protested, but he managed to force himself to be content. This woman in his arms was his to protect. She would be Pixie's mother and the mother of his other child. He could wait until morning for more.

Rusty couldn't. She tried. But the sun was still cowering behind the mountain when she gave up her battle and began a shy assault with her lips on Cade's chest.

"What!" He came suddenly awake. He was being kissed. He was being fondled. He was already hard. Rusty was still asleep. She didn't know what she was doing. He groaned. He didn't think he could lie there and let her touch him any longer.

"About that assignment," she whispered, and burrowed beneath him. "I believe in getting an early start."

When Rusty woke the next time, she was alone in the bed. Letty was pulling the drapes and announcing that the doctor was downstairs to check her out.

"Doctor? Why? I'm fine. I've never been better."

"I can understand that, but Cade called him at first light and insisted he come and check you out again. He seemed to be worried that something might have happened last night. Didn't make any sense to me, but he was determined."

Rusty smiled. The dear man. She knew what he was doing. When they'd made love the second time, he'd panicked for fear he'd hurt her, injured the baby in some way. She knew better. This baby was meant to be. He was strong, just like his father.

Rusty smiled and turned her face to her pillow. It smelled of Cade. The bedclothes smelled of Cade. She let out a deep satisfied sigh.

"I know what you mean, girl," muttered Letty, "but I think you'd better get yourself to the shower before the doctor gets up here. Cade may have figured out the answer to that bull's problem, but he's driving the doctor crazy with questions about his own."

Rusty came to her feet. She wasn't sore. She wasn't angry. She felt wonderful. "Bull? What do you mean?"

"Seems he wasn't falling from any tranquilizer. Doak missed him completely. After he woke up this morning, Pixie set them all straight. She explained that Pretty Boy came from Africa. He doesn't understand English. He was only scared, like she was when she came here."

"Pixie was scared?"

"Yes, until Glenda, the good witch, made everything all right. She said that Pretty Boy just needed love."

"Yeah? Well try telling that to the hands."

"She did, and you know what? A chorus of 'Mary Had a Little Lamb' was all it took. He's following them around like he was one of Mary's sheep."

Rusty looked out the window. There in the corral was Doak, petting the bull. She raised the window for a moment. Letty was right. Doak would never win any talent contests, but she'd never heard a more innovative rendition of the plight of Mary and her lamb.

"Your shower's ready," Letty said.

Rusty closed the window and headed for the bathroom, oblivious to Letty's mock look of dismay as she picked up Rusty's gown from the floor.

"Must have gotten pretty warm in here last night," she said with a knowing smile.

"Yes it did," Rusty responded with an impish grin as she closed the bathroom door. After a quick shower she slid into a fresh nightgown and crawled between the clean sheets that Letty had put on the bed. They were nice, but they took Cade away, and she didn't like that. Then she skimmed her nipples and felt a shiver of response, bringing back the memory of Cade's hot mouth touching her there.

"Send the doctor along, Letty. I don't want to hold him up. And see if you can keep Cade downstairs until after he's finished. There are a few things I need to know."

"As soon as the doctor comes up, Cade's going to call Judge Meekins. That ought to occupy him."

"What for?"

"To arrange for the wedding. He says it's going to be on Sunday. Is he right?"

"Cade is always right," Rusty said with a satisfied sigh. "Tell the doctor to hurry."

The wedding was held at three o'clock on Sunday afternoon, in the study. Pixie was the flower girl. Letty was maid of honor. Eugene was best man. Doak, the hands, Will, and Ann-Marie were all invited guests. After the ceremony and the cutting of the cake, the judge reached into his coat pocket for the marriage certificate.

Instead he brought out an envelope.

"Do you want this back, now that you're staying, Cade?"

"'Staying'?" Rusty said, a puzzled expression on her face.

Cade took the envelope and handed it to Rusty.

"I don't think this matters anymore. But you might like to have it," he said tightly. "I mailed this the morning after the Cattleman's Ball."

Rusty looked at the envelope. It was addressed to Judge Meekins. On the back: *to be opened after I've gone.*

"'After I've gone'?" Rusty read.

"I didn't know what would happen," he said. "I only knew that a piece of paper wouldn't decide it for me."

Rusty opened the envelope. Inside was Cade's contract, shredded in pieces. There was a note: *The only contract that means anything between two people who love each other is written in the heart. If you don't want mine, I have no need for this.*

"Oh, Cade," Rusty said softly. "You love me? You really love me?"

"I really love you. Didn't you know?"

"Yes," Rusty said, tears in her eyes. "I know. I just wasn't sure that you did. I—I have another order for you," she whispered shyly, "about that place for yourself, the one you wanted to find to keep us from destroying each other?"

"I've found it," he answered steadily. "You said the first day that the trouble you had was with government regulations, manpower shortages, and the drought. I'm no rancher, at least not yet. But I can deal with those outside problems."

"But I don't understand," she began, ready to tell him that the Silverwild wasn't hers anymore. It was theirs, and their children's.

"No," he insisted. "You run your ranch, darling. I don't know anything about it. I do know about building dams and pipelines. Paxton will put up the money to dam the canyon. Then I'll build a pipeline to carry water to the other ranches and irrigate your pasture. We'll all profit from a cooperative venture. What do you think?"

"I think," she said, sliding her arms around his neck, "that you'd better stop jumping to conclusions. We'll run the ranch, and we'll build a dam, and we'll build a pipeline. And we'll probably fight about it every step of the way. But what I have in mind for you right now is an assignment of a different kind."

"Oh?"

"Yes, a much more personal assignment."

"Willadean!" Letty interrupted sharply. "This is a wedding reception. I expect you to conduct yourself like a proper bride and serve your guests some punch and cake."

"Letty, darling," Cade said with a broad wink, "who made the punch?"

"Well I did, with a little help from Eugene."

"That's about what I thought. I don't believe that the doctor would approve of Rusty drinking that punch. Pixie, come here."

The little girl ran to her father and allowed him to sweep her up in his arms. "Listen, Pix, I want you to lay off the Tundra Tonic too. We don't have anything ailing us anymore, do we?"

"No, Daddy. But Eugene says that it's a good liniment too. Pretty Boy likes for me to rub him with it."

"Fine. But you'll be drinking milk with your cake and sandwiches. Okay?"

"Yes, Daddy."

"And I want you to be good while Rusty and I are away on our honeymoon. Mind Letty and Eugene and Doak, okay?"

"Oh, I will," she said eagerly. "I already promised Rusty. But, Daddy, why are you going on a honeymoon to Alaska? Eugene says that most people go to warm places."

Cade looked across his daughter's shoulder at his wife. He couldn't say that they didn't need warm places. They took their heat with them. Alaska might be in grave danger of a thaw, since loving Rusty could cause a major meltdown. Utah could become a tropical rain forest.

"I wouldn't worry, Pix," he said hoarsely. "I think we'll manage to keep warm."

And they did.

If the world's climatologists noticed a change in temperature in a remote section of Alaska just above Juneau, they attributed it to faulty equipment.

Back at Silverwild, Pretty Boy took his work seriously, time and time again. But nine months later it was the first calf, born of that first mating, that proved his value.

Pretty Girl was beautiful. She was taller, stronger, and more durable than anyone had expected. So was her twin, a magnificent replica of his father. He was christened by Pixie with the unlikely name Toto.

But neither of Pretty Boy's offspring could compare with another birth on the same day. Cade Eugene Wilder McCall weighed in at ten pounds. The doctor, summoned from Coyote Wells, said he'd never seen a first child more determined to be born. He didn't even give his mother time to get to the hospital.

Rusty didn't care. Having Cade deliver his own son on Silverwild was just what she'd planned all along. He'd accused her of casting a spell on their child before he was even born. She hadn't argued. After all, he'd never been able to decide whether she was an angel or a witch. And she had no intention of telling him now.

A few days later Pretty Boy's twins were brought

to the corral for Pixie to see. She was fascinated, watching both little ones trying to nurse. The bull stood to the side and appeared to be looking on with fatherly pride.

In the house as Rusty nursed their son, she felt a swell of warmth steal over her. Cade, sitting on the bed beside her, was watching with a look of intense pride and something else, something she couldn't identify.

"Are you all right, Cade?"

"Yes. You're so beautiful, so very beautiful. I never knew loving someone could be so profound." He leaned down and kissed the child, letting his lips slide across to clasp the other nipple.

Cade groaned. "I can't believe that I'm jealous of my own son. He's where I want to be."

"Oh, Cade. I think I'd like that too. Come to bed with me."

"But, Rusty, we can't. I mean it's too soon."

She rose and placed the child in a crib by the bed, covering him as he slept. She pulled back her wrapper, letting Cade see her full breasts, swollen and trembling under his heated gaze. "Yes," she agreed, "but you're a very innovative man, Cade McCall. I'm sure we can find a way."

They did.

But when Willadean Wilder McCall was born ten months later, the doctor gave Cade McCall a strong warning that Rusty wasn't a cow. She couldn't turn out a baby *every* year.

Cade said he didn't mean for her to. Though Pretty Boy was making every effort to populate the range with his offspring, Cade explained, he had no intention of following suit. Two more might be enough.

Then again, maybe not. For Cade knew that he and Rusty had unending love to share. Together they'd made Silverwild successful enough to provide for all the children that might come . . . and every day brought them a new adventure in loving.

Cade smiled and wondered how one day they'd explain to their children that their adventure had begun with a simple newspaper ad—and Eugene's Tundra Tonic.

THE EDITOR'S CORNER

What a joy it is to see, hear, smell and touch spring once again! Like a magician, nature is pulling splendors out of an invisible hat—and making us even more aware of romance. To warm you with all the radiance and hopefulness of the season, we've gathered together a bouquet of six fabulous LOVESWEPTs.

First, from the magical pen of Mary Kay McComas, we have **KISS ME, KELLY**, LOVESWEPT #462. Kelly has a rule about dating cops—she doesn't! But Baker is a man who breaks the rules. In the instant he commands her to kiss him he seizes control of her heart—and dares her to tell him she doesn't want him as much as he wants her. But once Kelly has surrendered to the ecstasy he offers, can he betray that passion by seducing her to help him with a desperate, dirty job? A story that glows with all the excitement and uncertainties of true love.

With all things green and beautiful about to pop into view, we bring you talented Gail Douglas's **THE BEST LAID PLANS**, LOVESWEPT #463. Jennifer Allan has greenery *and* beauty on her mind as she prepares to find out exactly what Clay Parrish, an urban planner, intends to do to her picturesque hometown. Clay is a sweet-talker with an irrepressible grin, and in a single sizzling moment he breaches Jennifer's defenses. Once he begins to understand her fears, he wages a glorious campaign to win her trust. A lot of wooing . . . and a lot of magic—in a romance you can't let yourself miss.

In Texas spring comes early, and it comes on strong—and so do the hero and heroine of Jan Hudson's **BIG AND BRIGHT**, LOVESWEPT #464. Holt Berringer is one of the good guys, a long lean Texas Ranger with sin-black eyes and a big white Stetson. When the entrancing spitfire Cory Bright has a run-in with some bad guys, Holt admires her refusal to hide from threats on her life and is determined to cherish and protect her. Cory fears he will be too much like the domineering macho men she's grown to dislike, but Holt is as tender as he is tough. Once Cory proves that she can make it on her own, will she be brave enough to settle for the man she really wants? A double-barrelled delight from the land of yellow roses.

Peggy Webb's **THAT JONES GIRL,** LOVESWEPT #465, is a marvelous tale about the renewal of an old love between a wild Irish rover and a beautiful singer. Brawny wanderer Mick Flannigan had been Tess Jones's first lover, best friend, and husband—until the day years before when he suddenly left her. Now destiny has thrown them together again, but Tess is still too hot for Mick to handle. She draws him like a magnet, and he yearns to recapture the past, to beg Tess's forgiveness . . . but can this passion that has never died turn into trust? For Peggy's many fans, here is a story that is as fresh, energetic, and captivating as a spring morning.

Erica Spindler's enchanting **WISHING MOON,** LOVESWEPT #466, features a hero who gives a first impression that belies the real man. Lance Alexander seems to be all business, whether he is hiring a fund-raiser for his favorite charity or looking for a wife. When he runs into the cocky and confident Madi Muldoon, she appears to be the last person he would choose to help in the fight to save the sea turtles—until she proves otherwise and he falls under the spell of her tawny-eyed beauty. Still Lance finds it hard to trust in any woman's love, while Madi thinks she has lost her faith in marriage. Can they both learn that wishes made on a full moon—especially wishes born of an irresistible love for each other—always come true? A story as tender and warm as spring itself.

In April the world begins to move outdoors again and it's time to have a little fun. That's what brings two lovers together in Marcia Evanick's delightful **GUARDIAN SPIRIT,** LOVESWEPT #467. As a teenager Josh Langly had been the town bad boy; now he is the local sheriff. When friends pair him with the bewitching dark-haired Laura Ann Bryant for the annual scavenger hunt, the two of them soon have more on their minds than the game.

Forced by the rules to stay side by side with Josh for a weekend, Laura is soon filled with a wanton desire for this good-guy hunk with the devilish grin. And though Josh is trying to bury his bad boy past beneath a noble facade, Laura enchants him beyond all reason and kindles an old flame. Another delectable treat from Marcia Evanick.

And (as if this weren't enough!) be sure not to miss three unforgettable novels coming your way in April from Bantam's spectacular new imprint, FANFARE, featuring the best in women's popular fiction. First, for the many fans of Deborah Smith, we have her deeply moving and truly memorable historical **BELOVED WOMAN**. This is the glorious story of a remarkable Cherokee woman, Katherine Blue Song, and an equally remarkable frontiersman Justis Gallatin. Then, making her debut with FANFARE, Jessica Bryan brings you a spellbinding historical fantasy, **ACROSS A WINE-DARK SEA**. This story has already wowed *Rendezvous* magazine, which called Jessica Bryan "a super storyteller" and raved about the book, describing it as "different, exciting, excellent . . ." The critically-acclaimed Virginia Brown takes readers back to the wildest days of the Wild West for a fabulous and heartwarming love story in **RIVER'S DREAM**.

All in all, a terrific month of reading in store for you from FANFARE and LOVESWEPT!

Sincerely,

Carolyn Nichols

Carolyn Nichols,
Publisher,
LOVESWEPT
Bantam Books
666 Fifth Avenue
New York, NY 10103

THE LATEST IN BOOKS AND AUDIO CASSETTES

Paperbacks

☐	28671	**NOBODY'S FAULT** Nancy Holmes	$5.95
☐	28412	**A SEASON OF SWANS** Celeste De Blasis	$5.95
☐	28354	**SEDUCTION** Amanda Quick	$4.50
☐	28594	**SURRENDER** Amanda Quick	$4.50
☐	28435	**WORLD OF DIFFERENCE** Leonia Blair	$5.95
☐	28416	**RIGHTFULLY MINE** Doris Mortman	$5.95
☐	27032	**FIRST BORN** Doris Mortman	$4.95
☐	27283	**BRAZEN VIRTUE** Nora Roberts	$4.50
☐	27891	**PEOPLE LIKE US** Dominick Dunne	$4.95
☐	27260	**WILD SWAN** Celeste De Blasis	$5.95
☐	25692	**SWAN'S CHANCE** Celeste De Blasis	$5.95
☐	27790	**A WOMAN OF SUBSTANCE** Barbara Taylor Bradford	$5.95

Audio

☐ **SEPTEMBER** by Rosamunde Pilcher
Performance by Lynn Redgrave
180 Mins. Double Cassette   45241-X $15.95

☐ **THE SHELL SEEKERS** by Rosamunde Pilcher
Performance by Lynn Redgrave
180 Mins. Double Cassette   48183-9 $14.95

☐ **COLD SASSY TREE** by Olive Ann Burns
Performance by Richard Thomas
180 Mins. Double Cassette   45166-9 $14.95

☐ **NOBODY'S FAULT** by Nancy Holmes
Performance by Geraldine James
180 Mins. Double Cassette   45250-9 $14.95

Bantam Books, Dept. FBS, 414 East Golf Road, Des Plaines, IL 60016

Please send me the items I have checked above. I am enclosing $_____
(please add $2.50 to cover postage and handling). Send check or money order,
no cash or C.O.D.s please. (Tape offer good in USA only.)

Mr/Ms _____

Address _____

City/State _____ Zip _____

Please allow four to six weeks for delivery.   FBS–1/91
Prices and availability subject to change without notice.

60 Minutes to a Better, More Beautiful You!

Now it's easier than ever to awaken your sensuality, stay slim forever—even make yourself irresistible. With Bantam's bestselling subliminal audio tapes, you're only 60 minutes away from a better, more beautiful you!

__ 45004-2	**Slim Forever**	$8.95
__ 45035-2	**Stop Smoking Forever**	$8.95
__ 45022-0	**Positively Change Your Life**	$8.95
__ 45041-7	**Stress Free Forever**	$8.95
__ 45106-5	**Get a Good Night's Sleep**	$7.95
__ 45094-8	**Improve Your Concentration**	$7.95
__ 45172-3	**Develop A Perfect Memory**	$8.95

Bantam Books, Dept. LT, 414 East Golf Road, Des Plaines, IL 60016

Please send me the items I have checked above. I am enclosing $_____ (please add $2.50 to cover postage and handling). Send check or money order, no cash or C.O.D.s please. (Tape offer good in USA only.)

Mr/Ms _____

Address _____

City/State_____ Zip_____

LT-2/91

Please allow four to six weeks for delivery.
Prices and availability subject to change without notice.